unfinished

By

Roger Simpson

Dedicated to Gretchen, Dana, Randy
and to Wendell Berry, Thich Nhat Hanh, Gary Synder,
Chris Stone and Howard Zinn:
Voices from the Wilderness.

ISBN: 978-0-9995562-3-8

Printed in the U. S. A.

Library of Congress Number: 2018936742

Layout and Design by Pizzirani Consulting

chapter one

Telling me that I had done it wrong, the incessant voice of reprimand never went away. When I was small, I was afraid to speak. Or if I did it was usually to say something that might–or did–get me in trouble. So, getting in trouble became my way of getting attention that I pretended was love. I reached a kind of ultimate trouble, ultimate punishment, when I practically flunked out my junior year at the university and joined the military draft without telling my mother and grandmother: my parents.

That's why I was sitting on a bus bench of cracked imitation red leather in the crummy part of downtown L.A., waiting for the loud speaker to tell me which bus to get on. A filthy, stained foam oozed through the cracks and smelled like nervous sweat. At the other end of the bench, somebody had left a worn-out hardcover, and out of boredom I leaned over and pulled it to me. It was a book of poems by a poet I had never heard of: *George Seferis Collected Poems*. I tried to write poetry in high school, and the teachers who lived next door always smiled and encouraged me though I guessed the stuff was pretty bad. I don't think I once showed it to my family, or what was called my family minus my Dad who died when I was five or six. I turned the pages and took a random look at a passage in one poem:

"Or perhaps no, nothing is left but the weight
The nostalgia for the weight of a living creature
There where we now remain unsubstantial, bending
Like the branches of a terrible willow tree heaped in
Unremitting despair."

I skipped and turned the page:

"Shieldbearer, the sun climbed waring,
and from the depths of the cave a startled bat
hit the light as an arrow hits a shield...." [1]

Sitting there, I realized the draft was my only option after trashing my grades. Like it or not, I was Mark Eliot, draftee, for the next two years. No escape. For two days, I've been living in a cheap hotel, spending my time in the mind-numbing process of being inducted into the Army: endless paperwork. Was this a bad decision in a history of bad decisions? Over the years, my mother and grandmother often asked me about my decisions, but they never sounded very concerned.

They'd just stop on their way to the train my mother would catch to New York where she'd spend a couple of weeks each quarter buying the latest scents of perfume for the department she managed in a high-class department

---

[1] *George Seferis Collected Poems (Revised Edition), Edited and Introduced by Edmund Keeley and Philip Sherrard. Princeton University Press, 1995*

store. She always claimed it was the finest department store in the world. I couldn't argue with her, what with the chauffer driven cars waiting in the parking lot. I was surprised my grandmother came with her. She'd been living with us fourteen years because her other five kids didn't want her and lived in and around Chicago. They were all better off and could have easily afforded to take her. I mentioned that to my mother often and all she said was, "It's my duty." She would never answer the question why her brother and five sisters didn't have the same duty. I think it would have been easier for us if she had gone to live with each of them.

My mother asked me if I was doing the right thing. What was I supposed to say? But my grandmother was quick enough to answer for me and said I really didn't have any options since I'd flunked out of the university. The way she said it was almost sarcastic. Then I got a quick hug from my mother.

I read the poem again and sort of fixated on certain lines:

> "...bending
> Like the branches of a terrible willow tree
> heaped in
> Unremitting despair...."

God, did that seem depressing when I thought about it. I glanced towards the parking lot; they were gone. Why

5

had I practically flunked out? With so many huge classes, the work wasn't that hard. Ever since my Dad died and my grandmother came to live with us, it was different. But really, mostly all I can remember about my Dad are the times I would hear him come in at two or three in the morning. He'd be drunk or sounded like it, and when she'd demand to know where he was, he'd yell, "Leave me alone, you bitch!" Then the bedroom door would slam, and he'd be mumbling in the living room until he curled up on the small couch. I'd fall back to sleep listening to his drunken snoring.

I never got taken to see him in the hospital when I found out later he was dying from the alcohol. Never even knew when he died or about the funeral until she showed me his grave at Forest Lawn Cemetery a year later. I'd just turned seven, I think. Come to think of it not being at the funeral there was never a minister to tell me to be brave or patting me on the back like in the movies. I never had a reason to cry.

But what I do remember clearly was the time he took me in our old black Ford coupe over the hills into Hollywood to a bunch of bungalows that faced each other with grass, flower beds and a long path between. I remember a girl younger than my mother who came out of one of them. She had light brown skin and jet-black hair. They had smiled and touched hands and then both looked at me and smiled as if there was something wrong.

I got a ham sandwich, a Pepsi and a Baby Ruth candy bar that looked like it had seen better days, from a vending machine and took them on the bus with me. It was full of volunteers and draftees and I listened to their nervous chatter until we cleared the city and the window filled with darkness: the vague hint of farmland with a house lit or the lamp posts of a small town now and then. I don't know how long it took, but eventually we turned west, and I smelled the sea.

The darkness of the bus was raising strange visions. I remembered almost every night at the dinner table hearing my mother say to me through the fatigue of her long day, "Why can't you *ever* get along with your grandmother?"

So many nights my grandmother would pout, and my mother would sigh and ask, "What is it, Mother?" And it was always something I'd done wrong, however small. And I was really a good kid. I was sent away to military school for two years after my Dad died.

But other things took the place of those dinners. There was the row of cots and the military lockers and the light from the flag pole and cannon on the front lawn filtering through the sheer window curtains. The dreams of running away and hitching a ride, but to where?

"Get your dumb asses offa the bus, double time! Form three lines facing me!" the sergeant was screaming. I felt sweat on my back, yet it was 4 a.m. and the air smelt like salt. "Keep in line you pussy whipped morons and follow me, *in line!*"

Then he shoved a Mexican or Puerto Rican in front of me. "This is your home for the next eight weeks, like it or not. I'm the one who's gonna' see to it that you dumbasses are turned into fighting machines in four weeks less than you're supposed to be here cause some pie-faced general made the wrong call and we're runnin' outa' bodies in 'Nam. You got it?"

We all half-heartedly shouted "Yes, sir!" back at him and for some reason he stopped screaming. Where did they get fools like this from? He called out our names and barracks number. Mine wasn't called until the others were sent running up the company street.

"Eliot, you're not goin' with the rest. Get your ass up to Barracks 4, one at the top of this street on your left. You're a Marine now. Move out!" I ran up into the darkness. My duffle was banging against my right leg.

How I made it through to the seventh weekend I'll never know. I'd lost the ten pounds I'd put on at the university. They gave us the weekend off until Sunday night at five. We got a week's pay. I had dreamed of a weekend in Carmel. I still had my civvies with me, so I could wear them into town. I wouldn't have gone if I'd had to wear a uniform. It was winter and there were lots of vacancies. I found a beautiful room with a fireplace just at the edge of town and a short walk to the beach.

I lit the fire and settled on the small couch by the hearth, letting the warmth flow over me until my eyes saw the fire as a dancing orange blur. Those seven weeks had been nothing but hurry up and wait, hurry up and wait, a real circus of fools. Officers and Non-coms—fools. One big bag of stupidity. No wonder we were losing in Vietnam. And I was one of the fools. School, what a fool.

Maybe my grandmother was right. I was a damn fool.

For two days I slept, drank some bourbon, ate real food, and daydreamed. I dreamed about the old Norwegian lady down the block when I was seven and afraid of fire. With too much paper in the fireplace, my mother almost caught the Christmas tree on fire and her fear was so strong that it drew me into it.

The older lady's hair was dyed red, but the gray came through. She talked quietly and slowly, gently held my hand over the warmth of her own fire. She said, "There, see. Nothing to fear." I kind of cuddled next to her and we

9

watched the flames for a long time. I almost fell asleep, but I remember how softly she spoke. "If I tell you a secret, will you keep it?" I nodded my head and she nodded hers. "When you grow up you will understand what I say now." She'd hesitated. "Never tell your mother." She'd hesitated again. "Your father was good. But his life was not happy." She'd looked me in the eyes for almost a minute. "Don't you be unhappy. You understand? Don't you be." I'd said yes but didn't really understand.

The tide lapped softly against the sand as I walked the deserted winter shore. Why were these memories returning? I recalled my father in the garage at his workbench so absorbed in building one of his rare wood and jeweled boxes that when I touched him, he jumped. He smiled even though my mother always seemed to complain that he was out there so often after dinner. I already sensed back then that he didn't want to sit at the television with her and my grandmother. That was our life. That was just before he got sick and died.

Later, at military school, the daydreams continued. I was riding my bike home after a game of basketball with a friend next door. It was just twilight and not the actual house I lived in. No, this was a neighborhood of two-story English Tudor-style homes made of warm colored stone and set up and back on rolling lawns with oak trees. As I turned up the cobblestone driveway, the brake lights of my imagined father's car had gone off in the garage and he was just getting out. He wore a dark blue suit and carried a briefcase. I rode up the drive, passed the large kitchen window where the light brought a wave and a smile from my imagined mother. Then he was putting his arm around my shoulders and we came out of the cold into a warm kitchen with smells of dinner being prepared. They laughed and joked and asked about school and offered to help with any difficult math problems, and really wanted to hear me read the English paper I had finished for tomorrow's class. I also dreamed about girls. We were naked and kissing. But the imagined parents made up a lot of the dream hours in my junior and senior high school years.

The grey silence of the Carmel beach returned, and I stared into the oncoming fog. I whispered aloud, "They really loved me," as if I hadn't imagined it.

The streets were nearly empty, and I found a courtyard restaurant that served Mexican food. I ordered two Margaritas with an appetizer of chips, salsa and guacamole followed by a dinner of beans, rice and melted cheese with delicious sauce over a steak enchilada so tender that it broke apart in my mouth. I was the only one there except for an elderly couple on the other side of the outdoor fireplace.

In the gathering darkness, I walked the quiet, misty street back to my room and soon fell blissfully asleep with

11

the sounds of the fireplace. I guess I've always remembered it as one of the few real happy times that wasn't a daydream. Yet, as so often, the nightmare persisted in reappearing in different forms.

chapter two

Sunday, I stayed until the last minute to catch a bus back to camp and it was just after five when I went up to the barracks. But I felt so mellow, I wanted to skip up the street. I was about to be slammed back into idiocy because when I entered the barracks I found everyone standing at attention by their bunks while the sergeant paced the center aisle.

When he saw me he shouted, "Where the fuck have you been soldier? You're six minutes late! Get your ass at attention by your bunk! On the double!" I felt unbelievable rage rising in me and couldn't figure out where it came from. Whatever it was, something shifted inside me and I walked slowly, not ran to my bunk. I turned around slowly, and he was in my face, his spit all over me. "I said double time, Eliot! You dumb motherfucker! Haven't you learned a goddamn thing in seven weeks?"

From nowhere, all of the things I had tolerated and all that I had restrained myself from speaking about poured out, all of my control suddenly was momentarily gone and I yelled, "Fuck you, you miserable, ignorant moron!" and shoved the sergeant away from my face by his shoulders with so much strength that I startled him as he stumbled backwards and would have hit the lockers or bunks on the other side of the aisle if one of the other soldiers hadn't caught him. The sergeant shook off the help and charged toward me. He tried to grab my shoulders, but I hit him hard on the chin with my fist. He fell to the floor and I shouted like a wounded animal, "Ahhhhhh!" as my whole body shuttered uncontrollably.

"Enough, Mark, enough!" My bunkmate tried to steady me, and I slowly stopped the shaking. My shirt was soaked with sweat and I sat down on the bunk. I didn't look up even though the shouting began again. I'd never acted with such complete defiance in my life and I felt this warming rush of energy going through me. I didn't realize the immensity of my actions of standing against abuse and punishment.

I was completely calm, oddly almost at peace, as the two MPs led me down to the headquarters office. I felt a sense of relief when one of them whispered, "There's a whole lotta people around here who wish they could have done that." I couldn't believe an MP would actually say that, but it felt good even though I knew I was in more trouble than I'd ever been.

It was Sunday night. The MPs waited with me until the company commander was called from his home. They stood relaxed and casual on either side of me, and I would have liked to thank them for their secret support but kept quiet. The silence lasted almost an hour. The desk sergeant pretended like he was busy and even the Officer of the Day, a young lieutenant about my age, came in, glanced at me but never spoke as he went into the commander's office.

When the major arrived, he was accompanied by the sergeant. He gave me a stern look and the sergeant followed him into the office. It was another forty-five minutes before the sergeant came out and directly left the building, ignoring me. The major called me in and pointed to a chair on my side of his desk. He didn't get up but threw a report across to me. "Private Eliot, that's Sgt. Gomez's report on the incident. I want you to read it and tell me if you think it is accurate."

I read it and then looked up at him.

"Well?"

"Well, he never mentions what provoked the incident. I had taken all the disrespect I could handle, and I just snapped. I know many in my platoon felt the same way. As to hitting him, that was a complete accident; I'm not a fighter and never have been. I was afraid he was going to tackle me the way he rushed at me."

The major sat up in his desk chair. "Eliot, the military isn't fair. The Viet Cong aren't fair either. Those are the facts. Hitting a non-commissioned officer in the performance of his duty, whether you thought it was his duty or not, brings some dire consequences with it. And that's another fact. Sgt. James is filing a recommendation for a court-martial against you." I couldn't believe what I was hearing. A moron treats you like shit for seven weeks and this was the result? I didn't open my mouth. The major cleared his throat. "I'm holding you in the brig for your own good until a trial date is set. Should be a few weeks."

"So, what's the crime for standing up to a bully?" I asked in a kind of subdued rage.

"Looking at it that way won't get you far. The crime? First offense. Probably three to six months and a dishonorable discharge."

"In a civilian court, I pay for my offense and that's it. Here I pay and also get a dishonorable discharge. Have you ever thought just how bad that might screw up my life, just because of the actions of one idiot I defended myself against?"

The major looked shocked and angry but tried hard not to show it. "You'll have time to think about that, won't you?"

"Fuck you!"

The major got to his feet and looked at the MPs. "Get him the hell out of here before I decide to take further action!"

The platoon had gone on a night march and the barracks was empty as I packed my duffle bag. The MPs told me that all my time including waiting for a trial would go towards time served so it was possible I'd be out in three or four months.

I rode with them in a jeep out to the prison. They didn't handcuff me. It was dark now and the ocean fog had settled down close to the land which was barren except for a few scrawny oaks in a landscape of dying grass as far as I could see. The lights of the main post grew further and further away and were almost obliterated by the mist.

The MP driving spoke as if the jeep was empty. "Almost ten miles from the main post. Guess they figured anyone trying to escape would be too exhausted by the time he passed through this dead grass." I knew he was trying to cheer me up but was too stunned to respond, the closer we got. I guess once again I'd been a fool and was punished instead of helping myself.

The solid iron gate opened slowly and before the jeep entered, I looked back to see the fog spreading across the fields. We stopped in front of a two-story building with rows of small barred windows on each floor. They walked me across the courtyard to the entrance and quietly said, "hang in there," as they turned me over to another MP who guided me up the stairs and into the building's entrance to a counter behind which there were a dozen empty desks.

The man at the counter took my paper work. He was dressed in red coveralls with a number in green on the back. "You the guy who decked Gomez, huh?"

"Okay, Arturo," the MP interrupted. "Knock off the twenty questions and just do your job."

Arturo ignored that. "Don't pay them no mind, Eliot. They gotta puff now and then." Arturo smiled. The guy was about forty. What would some guy be doing here at forty?

"I said stow the chatter, Arturo, or you'll be back in the mess full time on dishes if you keep it up."

Arturo took my duffle bag over the counter. "You get three of these coveralls, five underwear and tee shirts, socks and these rubber soled slippers." He glanced at the MP. "He's in 203 by himself for a day, maybe two." He turned to me. "You'll have a cellmate soon, but you go through processing alone. Makes it easier." Arturo extended his hand. "Good to meet you. Happy as a clam in no time at all." He chuckled and pushed over my new uniform.

Cell 203 was just like a regular prison except it had walls and a roof and a thick steel door with a small window that opened from the outside. The door closed heavily, and I was alone. I sat in silence on the bunk for some time. It was hard to believe that college had been just weeks ago, instead it felt like years. There had been a girl back then, not really all that good looking. The sex was clumsy. God, I worried for days about her getting pregnant. She wasn't like the girls I daydreamed about, they never were. San Francisco was just across the bay with its jazz and rock and supposed freedoms; most of these hadn't even been fringe experiences for me.

The cell was warm, and the bright overhead neon lights seemed to make all the white walls run together. The small window opened, and the guard said, "Lights out in ten minutes." I surprised myself by thinking I was dropping my regrets before they could really begin. I made my bed and crawled inside, staring at the light with my hands folded behind my head until there was a metallic sound from somewhere and it was suddenly dark.

How could I be a criminal? Two and a half years of college. But what had I really learned? College was just killing time away from home. What will I be able to do? Who hires someone with a dishonorable discharge?

I wanted to get away from that thought and imagined my small bedroom at the far side of the house, away from them. My dead father and his boxes. The Norwegian lady by her fireplace. The walls look bleached in the darkness. I put my head under the blanket and cried silently and freely until the exhaustion swept over me and I sort of slept.

chapter three

The bell woke me. It took a minute to remember where I was. There was no light coming through the high barred window. Dawn was the overhead lights coming on. In a few minutes the door opened. "Get into your jumpsuit, pronto. Time for PT in the gym downstairs."

Though the gym was large there were surprisingly few inmates, given the size of the building. Maybe forty or fifty at most, all in their socks and jumpsuits. Most looked pretty out of shape or had given up being in shape long ago; they sleepily just went through the motions. Afterward, we put on our slippers and walked in single file down to the mess hall. I took a tray of food to an empty table and sat down. I noticed that there was very little talk, as if silence was the standard form of communication during meals.

After breakfast, the MP who'd opened my door took me to the basement to complete my processing. When I was through, we went back to the second floor. "You're assigned to cell 210. Your stuff was moved over during PT. Roommate's name is Raul but he's called Dino. He'll be back from his group shrink session soon." My new cell was like the other one except the door was a barred door and you could see into the corridor and some of the other cells. I lay down on the empty bunk and closed my eyes. I may have drifted off because the lock being opened startled me.

"Marco, my man, you are one bad dude." Dino laughed and smile at me. "Poppin' an NCO is fairly heavy for a white boy." Dino sat on the edge of his bunk opposite me. He was tall and black and had one of those bodies that look like pure fat but probably were tight and solid to the touch.

I smiled and shook my head. "I've never been a fighter. Always tried to avoid it. More like a coward but I had seven weeks of bullshit and just snapped. Never done that before. It's wasn't like me."

"I assume you're waiting for your court date?" I nodded. "I've been through that meaningless shit and guarantee you won't see anything resembling your constitutional rights. It's a slam dunk: biff bam, thank you mama." Dino's hard distrusting look was gone when he laughed. "I got four or less months left on a yearlong gig. Hit a sergeant first then a spindly second John. I mostly got slammed for the lieutenant, obviously.

I shifted my weight on the bunk and sat up. "How do you stand it? You sound like an educated person."

"University of Chicago. Nine units to finish a Masters. And this place isn't as bad as you may think. The chow's better than they fed us at the main post. I watch some movies, do five miles a day walkin' in the yard. I also read a lot, my number one activity. Don't even have to leave this beautiful home away from home to do that." He stretched and at the same time raised his arms as if to take in the whole cell. "I stay pretty much to myself. Don't have a whole lot in common with the white boys or the brothers in here. Don't worry, I'll give you the five-cent tour and you can decide how best to spend your time."

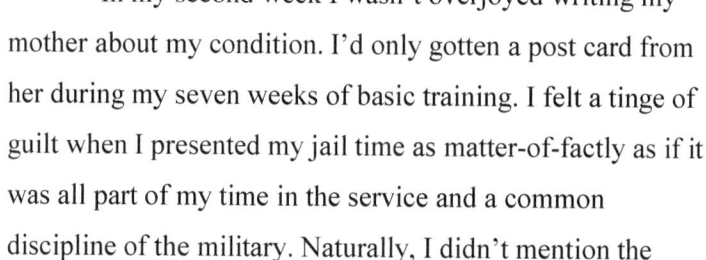

In my second week I wasn't overjoyed writing my mother about my condition. I'd only gotten a post card from her during my seven weeks of basic training. I felt a tinge of guilt when I presented my jail time as matter-of-factly as if it was all part of my time in the service and a common discipline of the military. Naturally, I didn't mention the discharge situation or hitting a sergeant. A couple of weeks later, I got a bombshell of guilt back from her which is what I expected. Gratefully no more followed.

My court-martial was during the fourth week and, as expected, there was no arguing it. I got four months with one month already served, and the dishonorable discharge. On the ride back to the prison, I realized that Dino and I would be getting out close to the same time.

Early on, he started giving me books to read and we'd talk for hours about them. I was secretly amazed that I could almost keep up with him and even contributed some good insights and ideas to our conversations. It was much like being at school without all the posturing, and I was really enjoying it which also surprised me. I'd never felt that good about myself.

"Don't believe the whole civil-rights-Martin-Luther-King-Malcolm-X thing settled it." Dino and I were lying on our bunks awaiting dinner call and staring at the ceiling. "Nothing's really changed, and we're well past the center of that first storm."

"So, it won't startle you when I say you're the first black guy I've ever known. The only black person in my neighborhood worked as a houseman for a wealthy family a few blocks away in the rich section." He gave a half grunt, half laugh. "Let me ask you this; even though you hit two whites, why didn't you protest that on a civil rights basis?"

Dino grunted again. "You still don't get it, man. Civil Rights doesn't work very well in civilian life and it's worse in the military."

He knew that I wasn't very tuned into the subject. "You're telling me that there's still schools in the South not desegregated? That few blacks can afford good schools? That minority opportunities in the work place are mostly bullshit? That few break out of that pattern?"

"Hombre, I can show you that shit in Chicago in jobs, the academic world, etc." He was silent. He'd gone over the subject more than once because I couldn't believe it.

We listened to a jazz tape Dino's brother had sent him. I confessed I'd never listened to jazz before. When it finished, I got up and did fifty push-ups. I'd lost another ten pounds. The jumpsuit hung loose on me.

"We're getting out at almost the same time. What are you going to do?"

Dino rolled to his side. "Take the bus to Frisco, drink some scotch, eat some Italian and hot Mexican food and pizza and ribs, listen to some jazz and in a few days ride another bus to Chicago. My old job at GM can't be taken away cause of the discharge—our union has real power. I'm not ready to go back to finish the Master's yet. Just gonna' smoke some dope, drink some beer, swim in the lake and build some cars. What about you?"

"I know I'm not going home, even as guilty as I feel."

"You gotta' somehow get way past that."

"Yeah, I know, just don't know how. I hope to ride into San Francisco with you, eat some Italian and hot Mexican food and pizza, some ribs and booze, say goodbye, assuming we get out close to the same time. Then maybe go back to live in Berkeley. Friends would put me up for a while."

"Maybe you can still get the G.I. Bill and go back to school."

"Hell, I'll have a doctorate in ideas from listening to you these past months. Don't know about the G.I. Bill, probably have to work, if I can get a decent job with the right hours and with the big assumption that I even decide to go back."

Dino smiled. "How do you know that all I've told you isn't bullshit?"

"Because most of it I've never heard or even thought about before." I turned in my bunk and looked straight at Dino. "Can I say I trust you? Look, I'll admit it. Nothing remotely like this has happened to me and I'm scared shitless." I rolled on my back and stared at the ceiling to hide my embarrassment.

Dino was quiet for a long time. When he spoke, his voice was quiet too. "You that honest. You'll be okay."

During the months in prison I kept drifting, unwittingly, into patterns that probably went back to childhood. It appeared in the form of needing to please, to be thought of as good, when I didn't want to please at all. It was a kind of ingratiation of myself with other prisoners. Each time, if he was around, Dino would keep pulling me back from that by either stopping me before I started or in the midst of the action. All he would say to me was, "cut the shit," especially when I was doing it with him, as if to gain some imagined favor. It was always, "cut the shit."

25

We were laying on our bunks again waiting for dinner. "Congratulations, you went through a whole day without doing shit your heart wasn't into. Amazing!"

"It's second nature to do shit when you've lived with it all your life. Not easy to stop. It still creeps up on me unawares."

"Well, you only just started to stop it. Pat yourself on the back for a change, as hard as it may be to do."

It was weird but when they let me out because it didn't feel like I'd ever been in jail. It was almost as if just another day was passing, not like a movie with tearful loved ones waiting at the gate. They gave me my civilian clothes to wear along with pay for the first six weeks when I'd been in boot camp; there was no pay for the jail time. The MP dropped me at the front gate where there was a bus terminal. Dino had gotten out a few days before. Besides the army pay, his folks had sent him money. I phoned him at the motel in Monterey where he was staying.

I didn't look back as the bus pulled away in the late morning fog. My normal self should have been worried or fearful, but I didn't feel much of anything. I told myself I would later when I was faced with finding a place to live and a job, but I just opened the bus window and let in the sea air all the way to Monterey. But that uncertainty began to grow with the ride. By the time I had walked from the bus stop to

Dino's motel I had an inkling of almost wishing I was still serving time.

Dino opened the door before I reached it. "Welcome, Marco." I was carrying the overnight bag with a toothbrush, comb, underwear and socks along with the books he'd given me that I hadn't read yet. "I like to see somebody who travels light because I already checked out and bought us some bus tickets. I know a pretty good small hotel in SF within walking distance of a lot of action. Remember, the first order of business is…. we're free! Never goin' back, whether or not Vietnam exists, I don't care. We're out."

Dino's older brother had worked in the city and given Dino the names of some restaurants. I knew where the Jazz Workshop was, though I hadn't ventured inside on my few trips over from Berkeley. He gave me a crash course in Jazz, and all the nights we were there we closed the place.

We found a street at the end of the Filmore ghetto where in one block we could get cheap, delicious Chinese, Mexican and Japanese food. I'd never seen restaurants like those before. Just storefronts with kitchens in the rear and about six booths, three on each wall. These were working man's places to eat cheaply with their families. Luckily, they were unknown to most of the city's population.

The first day while we were just meandering the city, I found a second-hand clothing store and got the perfect uniform for job hunting: blue blazer and gray slacks along with an Oxford button down white shirt and real silk tie—all for forty-five dollars. The three days we prowled the city Dino never had to say "cut the shit" once. But when I saw him off on the bus for Chicago, the doubts and fears seemed to dance out at me. I said to myself "cut the shit" and called a student and friend from my class, Dave Gale, who welcomed me to stay until his girlfriend, Annie, came back from Christmas break visiting her parents.

chapter four

The first day I was in Berkeley, I put on my new clothes and walked down the hill from Dave's and up Telegraph thru the south gates of the campus. On the left of the plaza was the Student Union, and to the right the concrete columned Administration building. Straight ahead, the law school, main library and classrooms were interspersed between islands of grass and trees. It was very quiet with the absence of most students. I suddenly felt I was back and almost wanted to be but had no idea if I would be re-admitted or what I'd study.

On the Administration second floor I asked to see a dean about re-registration. As expected, I had to fill out a three-page form giving my past grades, why I left, why I want to come back—I'd hardly been gone—and a whole slew of general information.

I expected a stern reception, but this dean was friendly and treated me like a real person—a big surprise. He smiled and just remarked, "So why?" We were sitting facing each other on my side of his desk.

"I honestly don't know. I was working two jobs but each day I told myself to go to class after work and ended up getting coffee and breakfast so there went my classes. I even enjoyed the class in English Lit."

The dean excused himself while he carefully read the form. He was silent for a couple of minutes and stared out the window into the plaza. I was worried whether he was thinking about my dishonorable discharge. As if reading my thoughts, he spoke, "The discharge is not a problem. If you remember, we separate education from the military. In fact, when Vietnam began, so many students protested that we were pretty much forced into getting rid of ROTC." He paused another full minute, almost as if he was deciding to say something or not. "I was luckier than you. I got CO status during Korea because of my faith, but it went a step further. I refused to do anything that was involved with the military, so my service was working as an orderly at a community health center in Oakland."

"That sounds very worthwhile."

He nodded and smiled again. "It was. Never knew how screwed up our national health policies are when it comes to being poor and/or a Vet. I always thought they were taken care of, but they're not."

"Sorry. I didn't mean to get us off the subject."

He laughed. "Don't be sorry. I'm the one who's drifting. Okay, back to it. This won't affect a decision but tell me about this altercation with the sergeant and the jail time they gave you. What do you think caused you to do it?"

It was my turn to laugh. "I just went nuts. I was sick of this moron shouting at all of us, spitting in our faces when he yelled two inches from our noses. Maybe it was the frustration that I was caught with no way out for two years. Maybe it reminded me of listening to something more mild but similar at home. I don't honestly know. It was so unlike me. I was taught to suck it in and follow the status quo."

"I would have loved to see that sergeant's face." The dean threw the form on his desk. "I'll reinstate you, but this spring you should concentrate on making up the two D's and the F. Try like hell to bring those up. If you don't, it will haunt you should you ever decide to go to grad school. You can come back tomorrow and register. I'll have the paperwork in the registrar's office."

We stood up and I shook his hand vigorously. I'd never been treated this nice by any administrator before. "I really appreciate your help. I thought I was going to be put through hell."

"I know it seems like that, but some of us manage to stay below the radar and don't get caught." He patted me on the shoulder. "Make yourself some good luck."

I sat on the Administration building steps for a while and watched a sparse number of people crossing the plaza. As so often happened, I started to find fault with this good fortune out of habit but Dino's "cut the shit" stopped me and I began to actually let that good fortune come into me. It was difficult. I was almost feeling like I deserved it. Why had I always rejected it when it came? What made it so hard to feel, to take in? I was always reaching way back in my mind to feelings that it wouldn't work out, wouldn't come true.

I'd register tomorrow and then stop by the Student Employment Office. With most everyone gone and maybe with some luck, I can find a job that matches my class schedule. I knew I also had to find a place to live which was always tough between spring and fall semesters.

I kept sitting there letting my mind crowd in on itself. Christmas just a short time away. I knew I didn't want to go home, even for a day. Hard as I felt it was, I would have to phone and tell my mother and except the flood of guilt she'd let loose. I thought about the poem by Seferis. I'd read it at least once a week in its entirety while in jail. The line, "The nostalgia for the weight of a living creature" seemed to have embedded itself in my brain. Dino had tried to explain it at least a dozen times, and a dozen times I hadn't understood it. If there was nostalgia for the weight of a living creature then the creature, man or woman, was a ghost, past, a dream, unreal. Suddenly the idea seemed to come from nowhere. I wasn't the slightest confident in my idea, but I thought that my life, especially at Christmas, seemed to have been a figment of my imagination. I was the ghost sitting with my mother, grandmother and my aunt and uncle who flew out every year from Chicago to celebrate— the only daughter who ever did. Sitting around the tree and fireplace, the lights. Eggnog with bourbon and my uncle always getting drunk. Then Christmas morning breakfast. Was I really a part of it, or was it only nostalgia? Sometimes it seemed like that time of year I could recall not being just the weight of nostalgia or perhaps only hoped I wasn't.

The next morning, I was back in the Administration building at the Registrar's Office. The woman who helped me asked what hours I preferred for classes. There were openings for the three classes I needed on Monday, Wednesday and Friday morning. She signed me up and I paid.

After that, I walked across the plaza and down to the basement of the Student Union to the Student Employment Office. The place was empty except for one girl filling out an application at the next counter. I always found the people to be helpful and nice there, no matter the crowd. A girl about my age with glasses came to the counter. "How can I help?"

"I'm probably looking for the impossible, but my best times for work are Monday, Wednesday and Friday evenings and anytime Saturday."

"How about driving a squad car for the Berkeley police?" She smiled. My mouth must have dropped open. "Just kidding."

"Happy about that."

"I recently got in some new jobs with the post office that should fit your schedule if you don't mind being a civil servant. Pay is good, twenty-five hours a week and health benefits. It's a new program specifically for students.

It sounded like a dream, but I hesitated. "There's just one thing that could be problem. You see, well, I got a dishonorable discharge from the service. You think that would eliminate me?"

"You and many other guys." She looked around the room as if a big secret was coming. "I didn't hear that. You didn't do anything really criminal, did you?' I shook my head. "Then I will deny this if it ever came up. Between us, I wouldn't even put it on the application. Seriously, they never check that stuff, especially coming from the university."

"That's a relief and I won't say a word. Can I apply for it?"

She pushed the one-page application across the desk. "There's a typewriter over there in the corner. Just fill it out and take it to the main post office on Shaddock. Supervisor's name is Dalton. He sees applicants in the morning from five to seven a.m. Okay?"

"Absolutely. I'll be there tomorrow morning. Listen, I appreciate your help."

She waved me off as if it were nothing. "Good luck."

Tom Dalton's office was grey from floor to ceiling. Besides the filing cabinets along the walls, there was nothing in it but a steel desk and three steel grey chairs. Tom got up and shook my hand. "You're impressing me already, getting here right on the dime at five. For most of your fellow students, it's quarter to seven."

"I've never minded getting up early."

"Well, the only day that requires that is Saturday morning because that day you work five to ten so it's a little hairy since you will get off Friday nights at nine. Think that'll be too hard?" I shook my head. "Good. So, here's the deal. You work the three nights during the week from five to nine sorting mail right here. Then Saturday morning starts at five when you sort a route. At eight, you deliver it and you get back here around ten or so. You'll have a regular carrier with you for the first couple of Saturdays until you get the idea of setting up your route. It'll be the same every week. So far so good?" I nodded again, wondering when he was going to look at the application. "The PO is trying something new. We're trying to give our regulars two days in a row off, Saturday and Sunday. Some outside consulting firm figured that out.

"Sounds like a good idea but...Mr. Dalton, don't you want to see my application?" Dalton picked it up, glanced at it and set it down.

"You get a feeling about people when you've been doing this as long as I have. Paperwork never means diddly anyway. When can you start?"

"Anytime."

"How about this Saturday at five."

"Great." We shook hands.

"You come in the rear door through the parking lot. There'll be a supervisor to guide you then. Hope it works out."

It was about six-thirty when I got back to the apartment and Dave had already gone to work. About 8:30, I walked down to the Mediterranean Café to treat myself to a latte. I sat outside with the early sun at my back and watched the people file by. Cody's bookstore was just opening across the street next to the gas station. I listened to its bell every time a car passed over the rubber strip. A girl with auburn-blonde hair shooting out in every direction like electric shock passed me going inside and smiled. Unfortunately, my half-smile came too slowly, and she was gone.

Her hair reminded me of a little dog named Squeaky whose hair did the same thing. That's what drew my attention to him in the pet store window with two or three other puppies. I would stop there after school, and work at the grocery store boxing and stocking shelves. There were always a few puppies for sale, but for these there was a sign, "Free."

They were happy to give me Squeaky. I rode home in the darkness with him in my bike basket. I got off at six, so my mother was already home when I walked in carrying the dog and put him down. He immediately ran over to my grandmother and peed on the rug. They'd been sitting in the two green chairs facing each other by the fireplace. They were having their evening cocktail. My grandmother let out a shriek.

My mother almost shouted, "Mark, where did you get that dog? You know your grandmother doesn't like dogs!" I remember pleading with her and she insisted he be given an immediate bath and put in the garage over the night. The next day when I came home Squeaky was gone. They told me he'd gone to live on a ranch in the valley.

I came back to my latte. The girl with the electric hair was back inside with her bare feet up on the table reading a book. I shifted my vision to the street again. They sold tickets to rock concerts in San Francisco and a line outside Cody's was already forming for a concert at the Filmore West.

I liked working at the grocery store. My immediate boss had been a jerk but the owner, Marty, was a nice guy, and the old bakery lady, Sara, always gave me one of the leftover donuts or bear claws when I came in from school. Until high school, I never wondered why I had to turn over all my pay, though my mother gave me some money I guess just to have in my pocket. Once I remember saving secretly for a special shirt the guys were wearing in junior high and how my mother refused to let me wear it.

When I looked back in the café, the girl was gone. Finally, I got up and walked into campus to examine the kiosks in the central plaza for rentals. They all looked like junk or share a house or apartment.

On the way back to Dave's I bought some lasagna and cherry pie to share with him for dinner. When I got there, I sat on the front steps in the sun and read a little of one of the three or four books Dino had given me. From the steps, you could look across Berkeley at the distant bay, Treasure Island and further at the tops of buildings in San Francisco—ghostly images in a thin veil of fog.

The book was about Zen Buddhism. I'd read half of it and understood less, but there was a chapter on meditation I decided to read a third time. I'd never thought of sitting in silence and trying to watch my thoughts go by. Dino said it wasn't easy and some people practiced for years and still didn't achieve anything.

When I finished the chapter, I put the book down and closed my eyes, trying to meditate, trying not to be pulled out into the sound of the traffic down the hill or jets coming across the Golden Gate and heading south to the airport. What was it supposed to do? What was the purpose? The writers in the book had spent their whole lives living in austerity in monasteries. Then I realized I was just creating more thoughts and tried to settle into silence.

I had no idea how long I sat there until I heard Dave's voice, "We can ship you south to Big Sur. There's a monastery in the hills."

I smiled. "Lasagna and cherry pie. I got registered and a job at the PO." We high fived.

"That's a good day's work to say the least."

"And I was finished before way before nine."

The next day I walked up and down Telegraph four or five blocks checking out bulletin boards until I had looked at all of them and came up with nothing. I went back to campus then and to the Housing Office, also in the basement of the Student Union. But I found either what I couldn't afford, what I didn't want or what was too big for one. For the first time, I wanted to live alone. I calculated what I'd receive from the PO job and I figured that if I watched myself and didn't screw up, I'd have enough and even begin to save for the fall semester, assuming I got more summer hours at the PO or a better job. I had enough to get into a place, assuming I ever found one.

The next day I decided to start early, leaving on my search when Dave was leaving the house. I walked up Telegraph until it ended at the campus and then turned right on the street towards the hills and the health food store and restaurant where I had occasionally eaten before I left school. To her credit, my mother had always tried to give me quality foods. There were only a few tables occupied and I found one by the front window and ordered organic bacon, scrambled eggs, toast and coffee. I told myself I couldn't be spending this kind of money all the time and was actually glad I'd practically been forced to learn how to cook; it had carried over and a balanced diet was important to me even though I strayed from it often. As I ate, I watched the passing students and others—some locals, sorority and fraternity students and some who looked like they were holding on to the thin edge.

When I finished, I walked up the hill to where the sorority and fraternity houses were located. The street split into islands of trees and well-kept grass. I had attended some parties up there, but the whole scene with its false bravado, macho bullshit and abandoned drinking had turned me off. I lay down on the second grassy island I came to. There was a light breeze and the few clouds and mostly blue sky filtered down to me through the branches. I laid there for almost an hour. The longer I did, I remembered Dino talking about being free. Before I got up, I did the yoga stretches I'd learned in a PE class first semester of last year.

I couldn't think of any other place to look on south campus and decided I'd walk through the plaza to the north side, even though it was more expensive. The thought of apartment hunting slowly began to depress me as I came down the hill toward the fringe of the business district. About two blocks up from Telegraph and near the health food store, the other side of the street became the edge of the campus as a fence and a border of trees. There was a man probably in his sixties I could see through the open door who was sweeping the entry hall at the bottom of a staircase. He also had a bucket of hot suds and a mop that he was apparently going to use on the linoleum when he finished sweeping.

From somewhere I had acquired the ability to strike up conversations in an open and friendly way with strangers. The man stopped his work and smiled when I said, "That'll be the cleanest entry way in town when you get finished."

He leaned on his broom. "Experience has taught me that if I make it nice for the tenant, usually a student, well, they'll keep it that way. So far, I've only been wrong twice in the ten years since we bought the building. Students are a lot better than they're given credit for being. It's all about respect."

"That's a heck of a record." The man laughed. "How many units do you have?"

"We've got two studios here, one up and one down, and a three two-bedroom complex, cottages really, on the north side. We live in one of those. My wife and I both worked for the government and took early retirement—no more hypocrites, no more working with people you can't trust. Best move we ever made and wish it was years sooner. Believe me, our units keep us busy."

"You...I'm afraid to ask with my luck, but..." I hesitated, "is this studio available?"

"For yourself alone I take it?"

"A big yes." He extended his hand to me and we shook. "Mark Eliot."

"Paul Horgan, come on, I'll show you, but keep in mind, there are a few others who want it too, as you can guess." He showed me a clipboard that was leaning against the stairs.

My hopes sank; there were at least twenty-five names on the lined paper along with phone numbers. I made a wish and signed at the bottom of the board, then followed him up the stairs. The stairwell was painted a silky white and I immediately liked it: no graffiti, very clean. The door at the top opened onto a generous sized room furnished with a combination couch and roll out bed with fairly new upholstery. There was also a comfortable looking rocker, a desk and chair by the front windows.

All the walls were the same silky white color. The floor looked like two by eight hard pine that was whitewashed and sealed. The windows front and rear were large, the front ones looking out on the street and across to the campus, and the rear looked out on a series of building roofs. The windows were large with east-west light. On the left of the far wall was a small kitchen indentation and to the left of that, a bathroom door. "It's got gas, so the bill should be fairly cheap even in winter and all the windows are double-paned, so it stays nice and warm when the heater is on. Just set it and it goes off and on by itself. You'll probably need a few kitchen utensils and towels for the bathroom, but that's about it. We ask that folks don't bring in any more furniture. This way it's easy for you to clean."

"It's my style for sure. Don't like clutter. And I'm neat. But this looks like way more than I can afford, even if I got lucky and was chosen. Right next to campus and my job is at the post office on Shaddock within easy walking distance. It's more than ideal."

"Well it's three hundred a month, no last month down payment and three hundred for cleaning which I put in an interest-bearing account—you get it back if we don't use the money."

"Are you sure on that price?" I asked in disbelief.

He laughed. "Do you want me to make it higher?" He kidded.

"It's just so reasonable."

"We know how strapped students are unless their parents are rich."

"Rich wouldn't be me!"

"So, we keep it low. The building is paid for and we make enough from the units and our pensions to do okay in retirement. We're not greedy."

"I'll say. When will the lucky person find out?"

"If you can come by tomorrow around ten, I'll let you know."

I shook his hand again and thanked him for his time. "I'll be early…. guaranteed!"

It was only nine-thirty when I rounded the corner at Telegraph and began the walk towards campus and the apartment. I was nervous and had the old feeling of "yeah, but." Translated it meant, "yeah but I won't get the apartment" which was really the combination of hope and doubt I'd lived with all my life. In other words, things weren't going to work out. Given the number of renters Mr. Horgan could choose from, I wanted to delay disappointment, so I stopped at the bakery for a fresh cinnamon twist and small coffee. I nursed those until I got to the right turn and walked towards my destination.

Up the street, I couldn't see a line or anyone standing by the door from that far away, and the closer I got I saw I had been right; there was no one. I figured they were already upstairs and swallowed nervously. The downstairs door was open, and I slowly climbed the stairs. The door to the studio was ajar. There was someone rustling inside. I

44

almost felt like I was breaking in as I entered and saw Mr. Horgan sitting in the rocker. He was holding the clip board and put it on the desk when he saw me and almost waved. "Right on time like you promised. Even ten minutes early."

"I can't help it. That's how I was raised." We shook hands. "When I didn't see anyone, I thought you'd rented it."

"No, and this is your lucky day. I started at nine and got two no-shows and three or four I didn't want. I'd say you got it by elimination but that wouldn't be true. I go with my gut feelings and share them with my wife. If she gets the feeling too, that's it." He handed me two keys and I wrote a check.

"I promise I won't let you down. And it will look just this clean when I leave, which I hope isn't until I graduate."

"Or find a young lady."

"It's not that that's going to happen but …. well, weekends?"

"We've got no problem with that. It's just the full time. For two it's a little small. It's been tried a few times but doesn't work."

"I understand."

"Guess I'll be going. Don't forget the utilities and phone. Our number is there on the desk if you need anything. Don't hesitate to call." We shook hands and he walked to the door.

"Thank you so much." Mr. Horgan nodded and closed the door. I walked around slowly, then sat on the couch and did something I hadn't done in years when I'd been forced to do it—I silently said a prayer of thanks.

I sent my mother a Christmas card, but decided my funds precluded a gift. Back from mailing it, I walked over to the north side to see how my old bosses were doing at the espresso shop. Even with its small business district, the north side always had a feeling of residential—almost country—to me, as opposed to the crowded push-and-shove feeling on the south side.

The café with its open brick front patio and wall-to-wall glass windows and doors looked different. The chairs and small marble-topped tables were gone. That was the area students had their drinks and studied. There was a neatly framed sign on the wall in yellow letters inside that said, "Tables occupied for a half hour only. Enforced." There was an older man behind the bar that I'd never seen before.

I asked, "how come the tables are gone on the patio?"

The man talked while concentrating on a drink he was making. "I took them out. Students sit too long, and I need fresh customers—turnover—to make this place pay. I don't know how the other guys made it." I wanted to say, 'because they respected the students,' but didn't.

"So, you own it now?"

"Yeah, did you work for the other guys? Can always use experience."

"Thanks, but I have a job." I turned and walked out. So much for this place. I realized again how lucky I was getting the PO job.

chapter five

When I woke Christmas Eve morning, I thought about the dream I'd had most of the night, or at least it felt like that. It was about both my imaginary family and my real father when I was about five; it was just before his death at thirty-three. Sun came through the leaded glass windows and touched down to circle the tree and huge fireplace in misty light. I didn't even try to imagine what my imaginary parents had gotten me, but I knew it would be what I'd asked for. Then my real father stepped out from behind their tree, smiled and gave me a larger version of the boxes he made. He said it was for special things I wanted to keep for a long time. I wished I had it now to put on my desk at the window sill, but I didn't want to ask my mother to send it. One day I'd go and pick it up if she hadn't tried to throw it out for a second time.

That evening, the winter light had grown into a subdued darkness when I left the studio and walked down to Telegraph and up to Dave's and Annie's. It was strangely and pleasantly still. The shops and the Mediterranean were closed, and there were few cars on the road. It was just past six-thirty.

I wanted to believe that I was relaxed, but I knew that would be kidding myself. I was going to meet a friend of

Dave and Annie's named Kim, and kept thinking maybe she
would be the ideal girl. Crazy. I hadn't even met her. I
glanced in a store window to see how I looked. Dave said
she was beautiful. Why try to set me up again? Last time
had been a super failure, yet the girl was perfectly nice. I was
getting the "yeah but" feeling and I said out loud to the
empty street, "cut the shit." I could see the tree in Dave's
window and swallowed with a nervous gulp.

    Annie opened the door and gave me a hug. Over her
shoulder I saw who I assumed was Kim sitting in the chair
next to the fireplace. Annie put her arm around me, guiding
me to the center of the living room. A new fire had just
begun to crackle, and Dave was in the dining room making
me a drink of Jack Daniels with ginger ale. Kim got up and
we shook hands with Annie's introduction. I didn't stumble
but felt like it—Kim was as lovely as Dave had claimed. She
was probably five-six, natural brown hair, blue eyes and
great cheek bones. That was as low as I dared look for the
moment!

    Kim smiled. "I hope they haven't exaggerated either
of our expectations."

    "Me too." I sat on the couch across from her. A
coffee table with dishes of appetizers separated us.

    Annie cut in humorously, "I didn't exaggerate either
of you, you'll see!" Dave laughed and set down my drink.

Dave toasted Christmas and we all clicked glasses. Kim looked with amusement at them and settled back in her chair. I noticed she drank white wine. "So, you used to go here?" She asked me.

"You could say, 'in a way.' I spent more time working at that new espresso place north of campus than in a classroom. It got away from me and I lost it." Kim nodded, and I wondered what that meant.

"But I can testify that he's truly an honorable man," Dave interjected, raising his beer glass again.

"Thanks for your testimonial." I added and they all laughed including Kim. The lump in my throat was moving away now.

"How does it feel to be back? How long were you out?" She asked.

"It feels great. As to how long, we'll need a couple of hours sometime to talk about that." What kind of an impression would she have if I told her? "I found a great studio and job, now we'll see how classes go. My problem is bringing some grades up and deciding what I want to do."

Dave had gone back to the kitchen to check on dinner preparation with Annie.

"I've had the same problem," She admitted. "I can't decide between nursing, a biology major, psychology or teaching English in high school. My Dad keeps pushing me towards law. He's a lawyer."

"At least it sounds like you have a few choices, all noble, I'd say." Dave took my empty glass to refill.

"Sorry to interrupt but I've got a late breaking bulletin. Annie and I will join you shortly and dinner will be served in about a half hour."

Kim and I gave him a round of applause, he bowed and went back to the kitchen.

"Do you have any ideas?" Kim asked me.

"Let's say I've had a lot of time to think about it in the last several months." I hesitated. "I assume they told you about my military misadventure?"

"No, not really."

I couldn't bring myself to tell her. I figured that would be the end of a very brief relationship.

"I'm sure you'll figure it out," She said encouragingly.

"I'm grateful I won't have Vietnam to worry about." I took a large swallow from my second drink. What the hell, I might as well be up front with it. She can either handle it or not. "You sure they didn't mention my military thing?"

"Honestly, no."

"I'm not ashamed of it. I did something completely out of character. I decked a sergeant when I was in Marine bootcamp. Believe me, a lot of other guys wanted to do the same. What worries me is the dishonorable discharge."

The look on her face told me that what I was saying was completely out of her frame of understanding. It was almost the look I thought my Grandmother would have given me.

"They let you back in school and you got your job at the post office, right? So far it doesn't seem to have hurt. Though I have to admit it's a little strange." I wasn't relieved, but at least I'd had the courage to get it out, even though I felt guilty. Then I remembered Dino's "cut the shit" and almost felt better.

Annie and Dave interrupted our conversation, for which I was very grateful. The rest of the evening during and after dinner was taken up with their senior trepidations on what they'd do when school was over in June, when was the war going to end and the protest scheduled in San Francisco the second weekend after school began in January.

Kim seemed easy to talk to, so I offered to walk her home but she had a car and would drop me off. We drove up Telegraph and turned right at the campus entrance. "My place is about a block past the health food store. There should be a passenger zone in front, so you could pull over." When she did I got out still with the slight buzz of the red wine and Jack Daniels which helped me to ask if I could have her phone, half fearing she wouldn't give it. But she did. "Thanks. Would you like to come up? The place is really neat."

"Maybe some other time, I'm only signed out until nine. I live in a sorority so we're neighbors."

"In a manner of speaking," I laughed and so did she. "I'll see you tomorrow then, different time, same place." I gave her a thumbs-up and to my surprise she returned it as I closed the door and waved.

The next day was warm for Berkeley at Christmas, and the sky was open and clear. We came earlier, had some eggnog with whiskey and for lunch Dave made meatloaf sandwiches, delicious and left over from last night's dinner. Then we watched Dave and Annie open their presents. I chastised myself for not having one for Kim but realized that was stupid since we'd just met.

Dave and I watched some football while Annie and Kim talked in the kitchen. They had known each other since high school and had lived close. I offered to give Dave some money toward the leg of lamb they'd made for our dinner, but he wouldn't think of it. With the lamb we had a light gravy, mashed potatoes and peas with Annie's homemade apple pie and vanilla ice cream for desert. We were all pretty full afterwards and sat around dumbly watching football until about eight when Kim and I left, and she drove me home again.

"I've got some white wine if you'd like to come up."

"Sounds great but I'm only signed out until nine again."

She liked the studio and sat on the couch. I poured us each a small glass.

"You live in L.A. too? How come you're not at home?" She asked.

"Oh, just getting out of the Army, finding this place and a job. I didn't even intend to go back to school. Let's just say I'm not all that close with my family. The relatives live in Chicago and I live with my mother and grandmother."

"What about your father?"

"He died when I was about five or six."

She reached out and touched my hand. "I'm sorry."

"It's been too long ago to remember much."

Kim sipped her wine slowly and was silent for a time. "My Dad might as well have passed away."

"Is he sick?"

"No." She rose. "Listen, I better go."

"Maybe we could have lunch or coffee or something this week before New Year's Eve. If you have time."

"How about Thursday?"

I got up and put my arm on her shoulder as I escorted her to the door. "Great."

"How about New Year's Eve morning coffee? I'll just walk down."

"Thursday it is." I dropped my hand at the door. As she was going out she turned back for a second.

"I'm…. I'm sorry. I have a hard time talking about him."

"Hey, that's fine. No problem."

chapter six

Saturday was three days after Christmas, my first day on the job. I must have been tired, because the alarm shattered the silence like a fire engine in a graveyard and I almost popped out of bed. It was four a.m. with only a vague hint of light in the studio.

As I made breakfast, I felt a tenderness through all the negatives as I remembered how my mother always emphasized "a good breakfast is the most important meal of the day" and how she would make it so. And there I was in my dark little studio cooking some oatmeal with a glass of orange juice and buttered toast. Why couldn't that feeling have been extended to the rest of our lives?

The streets were barely waking up as I walked down to Shaddock. It was weird glancing into the quiet campus plaza—there wasn't a soul anywhere. It took less time than I'd planned for reaching the parking lot of the post office, and I walked down the side of the gray building to the rear doors. I went up the ramp into banks of glaring neon lights, rows of sorting stations and hampers overflowing with mail and packages that hadn't made it for Christmas. I hoped I didn't have to carry anything but letters.

I walked toward what looked like a supervisor's station halfway into the building. The man who was sitting on a stool at the standup desk had one of those hair patterns to cover obvious baldness; his hair was grown long on the right side and slicked across the top. He kept reading something as I walked up and stood in front of him. I was afraid to say anything like "hey buddy" because I thought he'd be angry if I interrupted him. Finally, he grunted, put what he was reading down and looked at me.

"You the new kid Dalton told me about?"

"Yeah, I guess so."

"He said you would come bright and early." His arm swung out, as if encompassing the whole interior. "As you can see, even the regular folks aren't here yet. You want some coffee, there's a machine in the breakroom through that door."

"No, I'm fine."

"Well, since you are so eager I'm putting you on a route that takes thirty-five years of seniority to bid into. One of the best. My name's Hamie, and you're Eliot, right?"

"Right." He led me further into the building and to the right where there were a series of small cubicles. "You're in number five, Donnie Matter is the carrier's name. He should be here soon. When you come in around ten you come up and I'll punch your timecard. Remember, some days we need you to work over if someone doesn't show up. Is that a problem for you?"

I didn't catch myself in time and said, "No, that's fine." Why didn't I say 'yes?' I didn't want to work overtime at all. I hoped I wouldn't regret it.

I read a stray magazine and sat on a stool until Donnie Matter arrived. He was both good-natured and talkative and walked with a limp. "Got that in Korea. It doesn't hurt, even with the tons of walking I've done. I do get some disability which always helps. Got this job right out of the service and been at this station ever since. What I'm gonna do today and next Saturday is sort of shadow you around and hopefully you'll be ready after that.

It took over two hours to sort and pack up the route. Donnie said it would be less once I knew the route. We were the first ones out at a little before eight. His route was only a short distance and took in part of Telegraph and some side streets.

Before we got started, he treated me to an espresso and a pastry from the Mediterranean Café. All the old-timers and the manager knew him. "Been coming here since it opened." His route was only Telegraph for a few blocks and the rest was streets lined with neat front lawns and wood and stone Craftsmen and Victorian-style two-story homes. Most of these were just single family, but a few were student rentals. "Eric Hoffer use to say something like 'where there are students there are dogs,' but I think he called them 'kids.' Anyway, that's where the dogs are mostly. You got your spray, so you shouldn't have any trouble. I've only been bit three times in twenty-nine and three-quarter years and never in this neighborhood." I was relieved to hear that and afraid to admit I didn't know who Eric Hoffer was. I would meet his works when I later took a seminar on government ideology.

We took our time doing the route and he introduced me to a lot of people whose names I never got or couldn't remember. "In a few weeks this will be easy for you. The main thing is, don't hurry. If you do, you'll run out of work, especially on Saturday, and you might run into one of these idiot managers who tend to cruise the streets to see where you are. So, my advice is coffee first then the route slowly and relaxed. That way you'll get through right on time. Another thing, don't stray from the route area. That's a definite no-no."

We got back to the station with five minutes to spare. We said goodbye and he complimented me on how I was doing. When I walked out, Hamie didn't have any routes left over so I was home a little after eleven. My phone was ringing but I couldn't get to it. I showered and made lunch and was eating it at the desk by the window when it rang again. It was Kim and she sounded like she'd been crying.

"I just called. I'm sorry to bother you."

"You're not. How can I help?"

She almost stuttered and cried again. "It's...I hardly know you, but I don't have anyone in the house who I can really talk to and I feel dumb calling you since we hardly know each other."

"That's okay. I'm happy to talk. Who knows, maybe it's good that I am a sort of stranger."

"Would you mind coffee at the deli this afternoon around two? I'll ring your bell. I just felt you were easy to talk with."

"That's fine."

She thanked me and hung up. Odd since she hadn't seemed unhappy at Dave's and Annie's.

I began to read a little book that Dino had given me called *Riprap and Cold Mountain Poems* until she rang my bell. As I came down the stairs, she looked sad and her face and nose were blotched with traces of redness from where she'd been crying. I seemed to naturally have a caring nature from somewhere, and I hugged her. It surprised me when she returned it. That made me both uneasy and wondering if it would grow, a premature thought, I admit.

We found a quiet table by the window, so no one would hear or disturb us. We ordered lattes and I looked at her as she stared into the street like she preferred silence. Even with the mascara gone, and more tears, I was struck with how good she looked. I waited.

She turned to me with a small smile. "Thanks for getting together. I decided at the last minute to fly home tonight."

"That'll be nice for your folks."

"I'd just as soon not go, but they're the reason I'm going." She shook her head in frustration. "I'm sure I'm being stupid...but somehow my being there might help.

We sipped our lattes. For once I kept my advice and judgements to myself, a miracle for me.

"I probably am wasting your time. Maybe this whole thing is a wasted effort."

"Mind if I ask what this is about?"

Kim stopped herself from crying. She reached out and touched my hand again and then quickly withdrew it. "My Dad's been seeing somebody from his law office. I know who the person is and she's much younger. Oh hell, he and the girl both piss me off! Twenty-four years of marriage and suddenly he wants to be young again. And to heck with my Mom's feelings."

"Have you talked to Annie?"

"I just don't want it spread around...I'm...look, I'm ashamed. Annie's wonderful, but has a tendency to 'share' things with other people."

"But Kim, you haven't done anything wrong."

"I know but I just feel that way for some reason."

"Were things okay when you were growing up?"

61

"I always thought so. I got support and love from both of them."

"That's big."

"I guess it wasn't enough, both of them giving. I guess this has gone on for quite a while."

"Is there anything I can do for you?"

"Not really. Just this time is enough. I've needed to talk to someone who is distanced from it, and for some reason I think I can trust you."

"Thank you. I am trustworthy." The silence rose again and lasted for several minutes. Finally, she broke it. "I have to go." She got up abruptly and drained her cup. "I'll be back the day after the holiday. I'll call you. I thought I could talk but I can't."

"Be lucky you've got love and support. I had to create imaginary parents to find that."

"What do you mean?"

"I had a day-dreamed family. We had a nice house and they gave me tons of love and emotional support."

Kim stared at me in surprise. "Honestly," I said, trying to make light of it. She looked at me for a full minute like she might cry, but then bent over and kissed my cheek. She touched my shoulder, smiled, then turned and walked out, leaving me to touch my cheek and wonder how all that happened. And why would she pick me?

chapter seven

The next day I awoke feeling very much alone. I wasn't going to Dave's for New Year's since I had no one I wanted to go with. Kim was the only one I knew. I wasn't doing too much of anything socially until she got home. I had two weeks of groceries until my first PO check and a couple hundred left from my military, by some miracle. I wouldn't start my full assignment alone at the PO until after the New Year. There was nothing in my life but being right where I was. That had a scariness to it. What was 'right where I was?' I stayed in bed and took inventory.

I had the books Dino had given me. There was the new radio I'd bought for music. I could walk down to the health food store or Mediterranean and sit watching the people for a while. I could take some hikes up in the hills of north campus. I could walk over to the bookstore and buy the books for next semester and have even less money left. I could sleep late to kill some time. And that was it.

I decided to walk over and get the books since I knew they'd be out already. It was amazing going in there with just me and the clerks. Otherwise the place was empty. I found what I needed and walked to the counter without having to wade through a crowd or stand in an endless line. I'd already looked through the Anthropology and Sociology texts and didn't feel like looking at the novels for the other

class. So, when I got home I put them all on the floor next to
the desk, excusing myself with the rational that I didn't
know the assignments yet.

I spent the next two or three days before New Year's
Eve getting used to loneliness—truly a new experience. To
be honest, I thanked my mother for dispelling that feeling
with each meal I prepared and sat down to. Being able to put
something good together, then sit and enjoy it with some
wine or a beer took the hard edge off the loneliness. Her
forcing me to watch her cook, I admit, was what did it.

During this time, I even tried to write a poem or two
but realized I was just copying the poet who composed
Riprap. And when I wasn't doing that, I kept reading the
book over and over and interspersed that with a dozen
readings of Seferis's poem. Slowly over these days they
were both beginning to take some shape in my mind. I found
the heavy burden of regret of a lifetime lived in power but
soon forgotten in Seferis's poem. It was as if what had been
captured was that our lives were lived in an unconscious
regret and then, no matter how powerful—king or corporate
president or senator—they were soon forgotten. There was
Lincoln, once so powerful, sitting high above the tourists in
his memorial but now just stone passed by many people who
only knew him by a name, not the man.

Yet Gary Snyder's *Riprap* set forth a series of poetic
adventures in foreign countries and the backcountry of

America, the land of forest, sea and mountains. The poet
seemed to have lived these adventures. Unlike Lincoln or
other figures of power, these adventures gave a kind of
definition of freedom, of living a life the poet wanted to live.
God, I identified with that, and had since high school where I
felt isolated, though popular. I wanted to sleep in a hammock
on the deck of a ship with the breeze blowing around me or
wander the streets of a small Spanish fishing village at dawn
looking for bitter coffee and some breakfast. I could conjure
up dozens of such images as I stared, sometimes for an hour
or more, out my window and across the street at the campus
fence and its tightly clustered trees of the university's outer
western boundary.

I had nothing to accompany those wandering
daydreams until now and *Riprap* was the first actual book
that was making it come alive. But what did it mean in my
life? In high school, it had always ended with "yeah, but"
when there had been no Dino's "cut the shit" to buoy me up
and push away the punishment of the negative so creepy I
never saw it coming or from where it came. Here was
someone who hadn't just written poems about one of my
daydreams.

The phone rang into the silence. I reluctantly
reached for it. "Hello." It was Kim who I didn't expect to
hear from until she was back from L.A. I could feel tears
being held back. She was okay but just wanted to hear what I

was doing. Wow, that made me feel so good. But maybe
there was trouble. No, things were going okay so far. She
wouldn't be back until the middle of next week. She just
wanted to say hello. I told her briefly what I'd been up to,
and asked if she wanted to talk about her parents but she said
no, though I felt she'd called to talk about that. She said
"take care" in the sweetest way. Even back in high school I
was always running away from something. I didn't want to
run from her.

It really started when I was five and my Dad was
alive. It was a Sunday, and I walked out and sat down in my
bathrobe and pajamas on the pathway to the front door. This
could have been imagination, but I have always carried a
mental picture of my Dad talking me out of running away.
Putting his arm around me and saying everything was going
to be all right. Then we went in for bacon and waffles.

Most runaway times had been me gathering my
money and riding to the store where I worked and buying a
coke, some candy and pastries and riding aimlessly around
the neighborhood until dark. But there was only a wished-for
freedom in that, even if it wasn't real. Would it be real now,
like the poet? I didn't know what I'd be running for or to.
By the day after New Year's, I had practically memorized
the Greek poet's poem. In a few days, Kim would be back
and then school.

chapter eight

The sky was slightly overcast with cloud formations, but the sun was warm for early January as I walked to work Monday, the second of the month. The streets were beginning to fill with the spring semester which began the following Monday.

The next Saturday, Donnie had me sort and pack our route and I did it with few mistakes. We got out the door again just before eight but now the streets were crowded as we walked up to Telegraph to begin the route. We did our coffee stop at the now jammed Mediterranean café and I re-met the owner, Angelo Fuchano. He was a small man with dark skin, a large belly and his coal black hair looked like it was still twirling around and couldn't find a place to settle.

Angelo was all open arms and smiles. "You get my mail here on time and you never know when coffee and pastry are on the house."

"Thank you," I said. "But I'm only here Saturdays."

"That's good enough. Rest of the week, I got Donnie." He waved us off and went back into the kitchen.

This time, Donnie gave me a kind of rundown on different people on his route. Some of them like Jason Ricker had jobs I didn't know existed. He shared space with a tailor on Telegraph and repaired old cameras. I'd never heard of an old camera being repaired. Probably, the most

far-out resident lived upstairs in the building next to Cody's.
She was always waiting for Donnie in the doorway. Her last
name was Kasha and it was 'Miss' though she was a trifle
beyond that in years. She gave me a smile that could have
undressed both of us, took her mail and disappeared behind
the door whose glass was etched "Madame Kasha,
Fortunes." As we walked away, I didn't have to ask. Donnie
was ready to clue me in.

"She has been there at least ten years. Actually,
makes a living. Of course, she has other skills too."

"Like?"

"She's what I guess you could call an undercover
hooker." Believe it or not, that was just what I was thinking.
And that's how our last Saturday together went. By the time
we got back to the station I had a world of names,
characteristics and faces. It was going to take me some time
to get to know them all.

chapter nine

The phone rang. I was at the desk re-reading one of the assigned books for the literature class, though I had read it in another class as a freshman. I was never much of a reader until then, but it had started me reading. I'd had the same instructor last semester when I got the D, but she was giving it to us for deeper analysis than I'd had as a freshman. She would probably bring up the obvious idea of "the catcher in the rye" as a Christ figure. In freshman year, that had stood out for me and I'd had a dream of catching the little kids before they ran off the cliff. I thought then and still do that it would be wonderful to make such a difference in the world. I picked up the phone to call Kim.

"Hi, this is Mark."

"It's me."

"Hi. If you're not too tired from the flight, why not stop over around six. I'll make a salad and we'll have hamburger and creamed spinach."

"Best offer I've had all day. I wanted you to know it wasn't that I didn't want to talk when I called you, but it was just that my folks where in the living room too."

"That's what I figured. We can talk tonight."

"I'm anxious to see how you cook hamburger!" She laughed and hung up.

I straightened up the house, then ran down to the bakery in the health store for a couple of pieces of so-called healthy cake. After I'd showered, I got things ready in the kitchen and opened a bottle of red wine, probably rot gut, but all I could afford right then. I was re-reading the Seferis poem for the umpteen time when the doorbell rang at exactly six.

It was the first time I had seen her with her hair in a ponytail. It was a whole new look and was beautiful, accentuating her cheek bones and lips. She gave me a hug and we kissed hello, this time, surprisingly, on the lips. "Did we miss each other?" she asked.

"Yes, we did miss each other." I laughed. "Come in. The wine is probably not great but it's my best effort right now."

"I'd drink anything. God, I'm glad to be back and school starting."

I poured us a glass and we toasted. "To my last chance. I've gotta do it this time." We raised and clicked glasses.

"How do you feel about making it this time?"

"Well, I've certainly had a lot of luck so far; this studio, my job." Kim said nothing, but grinned. "All that remains to be seen, but I want to hear about your trip to L.A. if you feel like talking about it." We both leaned against opposite arms of the couch.

She took a long swallow of wine and was quiet for what seemed like five minutes. "Well, my Dad is offering me another internship at his law firm. And he's being really pushy about it."

"You never told me about law; I thought it was nursing or teaching English."

"I kind of always wanted law…probably because of him. You and me never really talked about that. I didn't even think of telling you—I passed the LSATs. I'll know in a few weeks about what school I got into. That's why at first I said I didn't want the internship—because of his fooling around with the girl in his office. But my Mom convinced me I should take it. And the two of them would work out the other situation. But I know my Mom absolutely won't stay with him, regardless of what she says to make me feel better." She took a tissue from her purse but didn't need it.

"I think I'd feel like your Mom. You know, a twenty-something year marriage and then this situation?"

"Why? Don't you think he deserves another chance? He was a really good father. I played soccer in high school and he made it to most of my games, for example." She paused again.

"That's why I feel for your Mom. If I was married it would be about trust. That may be old-fashioned after the sixties, but that's me." Kim looked at me for a whole minute and grinned.

71

"I had a hunch you'd be that way," she said.

"Well, I don't apologize. Same way I feel about drugs, old-fashioned."

She leaned over and kissed my cheek, but I didn't know why. "I'll admit, I do side with my Mom, but I also know there's nothing I can do. They're gonna have to work it out. Luckily, money's not a concern. I know he will take care of her."

"More than a lot of divorces can say."

"I'll live with her for the summer before law school; that should help."

"Sounds right to me. If you're ready, I'll make dinner." I pretended to be flipping a hamburger as we got up, poured some more wine and went to the kitchen. I couldn't get over how relaxed I felt with Kim. It was usually just the opposite with most girls, like I had to portray a kind of image of who I thought they should think I was. I hadn't figured out why, since I was a student body officer in high school which must have meant I was okay. Maybe Kim was just this shallow sorority sister I was glorifying into a deeper soul—like I often did without ever understanding why.

After a truly relaxing dinner we shared washing and drying the dishes. It even felt right to me when Kim stopped for a minute and kissed me, and I returned it. So easy, no real feeling of self-consciousness at all.

We spent the evening talking about high school and a letter I never expected from Dino. He was back at GM, listening to jazz and swimming in Lake Michigan after work. I told her what he'd done for me and like me, she'd never had a black friend. There were none in her sorority or in the expensive high school she had gone to.

It was a fancy, super wealthy school for girls that could almost guarantee you'd get in the college of your choice. She was only close to a few girls, Annie being one of them. The rest were always trying to impress each other with how many things they had, where they went on trips and the boys they were going out with. It really surprised me when Kim said she hadn't dated that much in part because it was hard to get to know boys when there weren't any around, and all the "making an impression" stuff got old fast. Looking as sweet as she did, I thought she would have been on lots of dates.

Her Mom and Dad were both from families who had been in L.A. for generations, so she recalled that money had never been a big deal nor did her parents put any emphasis on it. But it had meant a lot to me since we didn't have much, and I wondered how it would really affect our relationship, since that's what I felt was beginning.

"In my home, it was just the opposite, probably because it was just my Mother who worked, and she got no financial help from most of my aunts and uncles to take care of the grandmother. It was mostly just one from Chicago who helped but I don't know how much. Growing up, I also remember that every so often my Grandmother would chime in, saying how my Dad had been fairly good for nothing, never leaving anything when he died. I couldn't understand why my Mother never defended him when the she talked that way."

"Who really liked your Dad?"

"Me, I guess. But that's only memories." She slid across the couch and leaned against my shoulder. I turned her face to me and gave her a long, gentle kiss on the lips. She turned fully toward me and returned it, but this time her tongue shot between my lips and I couldn't help getting excited, which I tried to hide.

She smiled teasingly. "I think I just felt Charlie Brown say hello." I must have gotten beet red and we both laughed and rested back against the couch.

"Yeah, that's dear old Charlie," and we laughed again. "So, shall we change the subject and I'll tell you my pathetic high school story? Somewhat of another failure."

Kim nodded. "But I doubt if it was a failure."

"It's a very short story. I played football, which I hated, and you were considered a loser if you didn't go out for the team. What I loved was tennis, and I was good at it."

"Me too," she interrupted.

"Great, we've got a sport in common. Anyway, I was doing okay, getting three A's and two B's as we came to the end of the senior year. There was a rule that seniors could sit in their cars during study hall hours and I'd smoke an occasional cigarette out there in the parking lot. But some of the guys were drinking wine and one of these guys going home almost hit the wife of some big shot who called the school and raised hell. I guess that scared the headmaster, and he called us in and said he knew who did it, which was a lie, and we had until Friday to report to him. I was one of the first and confessed about the smoking. Finally, most of the others who had been drinking came forward too but instead of separating what we had done—I was legally smoking age and they weren't legally drinking age—he gave us all two weeks off just before finals. The same punishment."

"That wasn't fair."

"I mentioned that to my Mother, but she was so upset that it didn't register. Yet the worse part was that the teachers were left to grade us as they pleased. I was always expressing my opinions, dumb as some may have sounded, which of course was a no-no. I guess I was somewhat of a big mouth—but respectful—so they graded subjectively. I aced all my exams but got graded down, so I ended up with three B's and two C's which killed any chance of getting in on scholarship to an eastern school. But I was okay for Cal, and don't regret coming here."

"Well, unlike you," Kim pointed comically at my chest, "I really wanted to come here so whatever you think, you weren't a failure coming here."

"I agree. I agree."

Kim got up and finished her wine, taking both our glasses to the sink. "It's twenty to nine and I'm only signed out until then."

I helped with her sweater and threw on my jacket. "You don't have to walk me home. I'll be okay."

"Fat chance of that." We walked slowly up the partially darkened street. Our hands seemed to anticipate each other as we walked up the brick path to her sorority. We stopped on the porch. "That was a lot of fun." Kim put her arms around my neck. "That was rotten what happened in high school."

"Yeah, and I'm trying to put it behind me."

"On the bright side, there's us." She pulled me towards her and gave me a vigorous French kiss that bought up old Charlie again as I pressed against her. "Oh, oh, looks like Charlie's awake again." Her laugh was quick and so sweet.

"Yeah, he picks the worst times to wake up."

"I'll hold that thought again! Call me or I'll call you." She looked at the door and then back at me. "You know, you're easy to be with."

"My feelings exactly." I said, jokingly.

Kim opened the door and I walked back, trying to figure out what was going on with us in so short a time. Was I worthy of someone with money? Sorry, that's just my conditioning. I can't help it.

chapter ten

We talked every day but didn't see each other, and that felt all right. The next Saturday after my route, I had a long conversation with the Psychic-Palm Reader. It took me forever to get away from her because she said I needed a reading badly since she could feel both immense power and great confusion emanating from me. She would open a channel to the Astral World, whatever that was, and it would open the new life I was just beginning. She even knew about my military incident and the jail time I had done. It was strange and almost frightening, but it also sounded weird.

I mentioned it to Kim when we got together for dinner and a foreign film in the city. She insisted on treating since I hadn't been paid yet. As for dinner, she knew both the expensive and the cheap places to eat and get an excellent meal in both. I thought some rich fraternity type had been dating her but was afraid to ask. She seemed to sense my unasked question and volunteered that she and her folks often came to "the city." Her mother had located the film theatre on one of their trips north. It was just a no-frills room with metal chairs in a typical middle to lower-middle class neighborhood and showed nothing but the latest European films by all the great directors. I didn't know any of them, even though Dino had dragged me to an art house downtown with the same films when we were together. On the drive home, she asked me to drive her Volvo because city traffic scared her. I bought up that fact about Dino and she wanted to know what it was like, being around someone like him.

"Let's say, he wasn't a sharecropper. A U of Chicago grad who had almost completed his MA in Sociology. A very bright guy."

"I mean…well, the race thing. I don't mean to sound like a southerner."

I couldn't help teasing her. "Nothing special really…. other than the stick that was stuck through his upper lip as a tribal initiation."

"Really!" she exclaimed and hit my shoulder hard. "Stupid!"

"Just kidding, just kidding. In truth there was nothing different about him. I guess you could say he'd seen all the civil rights bullshit. Like I said, he was bright. Lots of times I couldn't follow his train of thought too well."

"What doesn't he like about civil rights? I thought it helped a lot of minorities?"

"I don't know, Kim. He says it's mostly just politics, and the people who need help the most aren't and won't be getting it. He got me reading some black writers and a newspaper for the Nation of Islam. He thinks even those people don't get it, and they're black." I shook my head in frustration. "I don't know."

"He must be kind of radical if he reads the <u>Nation of Islam</u>. They're really radical. One of them, Malcolm X, was killed by his own people and he was high up in the group."

"One of the papers Dino gave me had an old article by Malcom X. He was very articulate. He sounded like he cut through all the politics."

"Maybe so, but everyone I've talked to seems to think he was pretty far out and that's why he was killed."

"Dino said he was killed because he told the truth."

"Oh, come on."

"Maybe he was telling the truth, I don't know."

She threw up her arms. "My folks were big conservative supporters of civil rights, but they thought he was radical too."

I shook my head in resignation. I didn't really have a viewpoint. "What's there to say?"

"Oh, I guess I'm just a dumb sorority sister. And all of us are bigots, anyway." I hadn't seen her mad like that before. She stared out into the darkness as we crossed the Oakland Bay Bridge. It was a very long silence.

"I don't think you're dumb or a bigot. Don't take it personal, please." She didn't speak until we were driving up Telegraph. She put out her hand in the dark and squeezed my wrist.

"I'm sorry. I guess I'm around so many bigots up here that I'm one too."

"No way, no way." I said. She slid over and leaned on my shoulder until we reached her sorority house and pulled over.

"I don't want to go in yet. Do you want to talk awhile?" I nodded.

"What shall we talk about?"

"Maybe not the race issue." Kim smiled.

"Okay, I have a subject, not about race. I have this woman probably in her late thirties who's on my route. You know the psychic on Telegraph? I couldn't get away from her. She insisted I get a reading. Said I was both dark and powerful and what got me was she knew I was kind of starting over at school and other stuff."

She smiled again. "I had one. It was really good."

"No joke?"

"But there's also something else I heard about her." Kim said almost in a whisper.

"You mean the prostitute thing?"

"How'd you know? Did you fall for that?" She teased.

"No, I didn't, the guy who has my route regularly told me."

"Well, I'm happy to hear that. But I do mean it. She isn't expensive, and you might learn something. But not the second part!"

"Coming from you, I'll consider it when I can rub some cash together." But I did want to close out our conversation by again bringing up race just a little bit." She looked suspicious but nodded. "Thanks. I only wanted to mention it. Dino also wrote that he's thinking of moving back to Africa."

"What on earth for?"

"He says it could be a real life not a half-life. He feels stifled here, even with civil rights."

"I don't know what to say."

"I agree, we'll take it up again, maybe." I got out of the car and opened the door for her.

"See you."

"Sleep well."

"Is that couch really all that comfortable?"

"Yes." I kissed her and handed over the car keys. "Tomorrow?" She waved to me as I walked down the hill to my place.

chapter eleven

It was a cold, wet and windy day at the end of March, and Kim and I had finished our midterms and were laying under my new dark blue quilt. We were both pretty used to the couch mattress and it really wasn't bad. I had already gotten two of my exams back with A's in the two D classes, so I wasn't "yeah butting" then. I was pretty sure I did well on my English Lit paper also.

I had worked hard thus far into the semester, though I still didn't know what I was working hard for. She had been accepted at USC Law School. She looked almost embarrassed when I asked again what happened to Nursing and teaching English. Nothing had declined or improved with her parents. It was still status quo and many of our conversations seemed to draw their history and present situation in. We were staring at the front windows as we talked, lying next to each other, an arm and a leg touching. Kim was talking about their love.

"I don't believe that they don't love each other. They always openly showed affection. When I was younger, it used to embarrass me when they'd hug and hold hands in public. And it was continuous." She was stroking my leg almost self-consciously with the back of her hand. She glanced over the edge of her pillow at me. "Don't you think we're kind of that way if not so much in public?"

She really was beautiful. The only makeup she was wearing was some eye shadow because I had once or twice off-handedly mentioned that her eyebrows were thick enough and almost auburn in color and she didn't need any make up.

"You're looking at me, aren't you?"

"Yes I am." I was rubbing her arm and my hand sometimes drifted close to her left breast.

"Do I still look alright without the makeup?"

"You know you do."

"You want me to repeat my question?" I laughed.

"No, I got it. Yeah, I think so. But you are affectionate."

"But not so much in public like your parents." I set up a pillow and leaned against it but was still under the quilt. I couldn't help it; my hand kept moving closer to the edge of her breast.

"You're losing your concentration." Kim smiled.

"No, just shifting it. I can't help it."

"I want to be serious." I nodded. "What do you think…you know, I mean, love means?

"You know there wasn't any emotion in my family. I honestly don't know. I'd like to think what we've shared during these month's verges on it. But honestly, you know more than me because I never saw affection growing up."

84

She also sat up against a pillow and stared into the swirling downpour outside. A cell had just come over and it was raining so hard that you could hardly see across to the campus fence and trees. When she spoke, it was almost a whisper against the rain hitting the windows. I moved over and put my arm around her. "I do keep trying. You can see that can't you?" She didn't say anything but signed.

She took my hand and kissed it. "That must have been awful for you. It…it's almost like child abuse."

"But you're not getting hit like common abuse. In fact, as I look back on it I never realized there wasn't any show of affection. I guess I just figured that everybody lived that way." I could swear that her eyes were moistening up.

"You were just this little kid with nobody to lean on. God, I was so lucky in comparison. I guess that's why I feel so bad about them breaking up; it had been so good for me…and them, once."

"Kind of like that little dog Squeaky that I brought home." I was willing to laugh it off.

"Yes, you should have slept in the garage full-time." She touched my face and I couldn't help but kiss her. A couple months and she'd be back in L.A.

The first real argument we had was in early May only a month before the spring semester ended. Maybe up to then, we'd just wanted to please each other. I know I did because I would often defer to her wishes and ideas. For me, that was as usual the unself-conscious need to please and forgetting the "cut the shit" from Dino.

Anyway, we had been seeing less of each other, not because the lamp had gone out but because she was busier with her final studies and maintaining her grades for law school. She was also helping the sorority with plans for next year's rush and summer interviews seniors like her and others would be conducting.

It was just by accident that we ran into each other on a freak rainy day under the overhang of the Student Bookstore building as she was existing and I was about to enter. Our umbrellas nearly clashed and we both stopped, recognized each other and laughed as we hugged.

"What's a nice person like you doing in an awful place like this?" I asked.

"I was selling back some textbooks I'll never use again."

"That surprises me. I didn't know you were on a scholarship."

"You know I'm not. But some of them are so awful I wouldn't want them on any bookshelf of mine. I'm a little strung out with the sorority and graduation approaching. I gotta go." Kim started turn toward the rain and I stopped her with my umbrella.

"No time for coffee?"

She shook her head. "Oh, I wanted to ask if we were going to the last dance at the sorority? I really should be there." Then her tone suddenly changed. It wasn't soft anymore. "I've missed quite a few so far."

"I know, because of me."

"Honestly, yes. A couple of my sisters even asked me why you were so anti-social." There was just the vaguest hint of irritation in her voice.

"But you know the reason."

"Yes, I know the reason, but I don't think you've given them a chance. I know there's a whole lot of shallowness and phony-bologna but really, Mark, I don't think you've given them a chance. You can't judge them all. Some are really nice." And then out of nowhere. "Of course, maybe you don't think I'm capable of telling the difference. In fact, that I'm really one of the shallow ones!" She turned again to go, and her face was red even with the cold and rain. She was about two feet out in the downpour when I grabbed her arm. She tried to shake me off, but I pulled her back out of the rain.

"Hold on!" She settled down and I released my grip. "What bought that on?"

She wouldn't look at me, but I could see the tears suddenly well up in her eyes. She stood looking away as she began to sob. I took her arms and turned her towards me and she almost fell against my shoulder. I grabbed her tightly and

87

awkwardly kissed her ear. "What is it, really? Not the sorority certainly?"

She must have cried for five minutes before she tried to speak. I got out a fresh handkerchief.

"Thank you." Kim wiped her eyes and blew her nose two or three times. "I'm…. I'm sorry. I didn't mean to take out my bitchiness on you." She glanced towards the rain as if she would cry again and then looked back at me.

"What is it?" I gently turned her chin with my finger, so she had to look straight at me.

"My mother called last night. I wanted to call but we've talked so much about it that I thought you didn't want to hear any more." I shook my head. "My Dad moved to a condo in Westwood, closer to his offices. He told her he's going to file in the next few days."

"Sorry won't be much help, but I am. Really."

She leaned over, pressing her wet cheek against mine and kissed me. We held each other for a long time, as passersby stared and the rain kept coming. "If you want to come over tonight for pizza we can talk. And I have an idea to offer. Six o'clock?" This time there was at least a half smile as she nodded.

It was hard to know what to say to Kim. The rain had stopped, and the sky was clearing when the pizza came. The silence outside floated in and around us as we ate and drank a glass of beer. I didn't know how to start a conversation about her folks or even offer the idea I was going to bring up, and Kim didn't either. I ended up apologizing for no reason and she just smiled and said, "It'll come up again. I'm glad we can have silences sometimes." I walked her home.

chapter twelve

I didn't realize that the week passed so quickly. We only spoke again on Friday morning and it was just to touch base, nothing serious. We were going to a local concert of Bach at the campus library the next evening, and then out for dinner. I was sure the subject of her parents would arise again.

The clouds had completely cleared when I left the station just after eight. The wet pavement and puddles remained, but the rubber boots I'd bought at the thrift store kept the water out. Yet even with the difficult weather, when I got to Kasha the psychic's door, there she was standing and dutifully waiting. She was dressed in a long purple sari and her hair had changed to black since last weekend. It was in sharp contrast to her skin which was magnified by the pale red eye shadow and lipstick. "A couple of letters but mostly catalogues."

She didn't seem surprised. Her brown eyes kept staring at me without blinking. "Today is the day, the arrangement of stars says." Even as she took the mail, she didn't stop staring.

"I don't get it Kasha. You know I'm a student and can't afford seventy-five bucks."

She waved her hand in front of her, palm out, as if to stop the words. "You need this, Mark. How about twenty-five?"

"Yeah, I could make that."

"Be here at noon. And bring us lunch. Two teas and two hot pastrami and cheese on French rolls from the deli at the corner. All right?"

"You're sure I need this?"

"You will see."

"What if they make me work overtime?"

"If they do, will you be free at five?

"Definitely."

I had no idea what I was letting myself in for, and settled it to the back of my mind until I finished the route. This time, Haime was waiting. "We had a sicko today. I need you to take it. Shouldn't be more than a couple of hours. You take the number twenty-three bus down at the corner and it'll drop you off where you pick up the twenty-eight. Then ride the twenty-eight to fourth street. The driver will let you know where to get off and where to pick you up back to the twenty-third. The route is in cubicle C and it's already sorted. All you have to do is deliver. Piece of cake."

The way he said that made me detect a kind of weariness in his voice, but I didn't think anything of it then. I packed up and walked to the bus. The driver of bus twenty-three was full of conversation and good spirits until I told him where I was going. But then he sighed, shook his head and whistled. We were the only ones on the bus. "Man, somebody doesn't like you or, maybe, doesn't care."

"What do you mean?"

"That's smack in the middle of the worst Oakland housing project and it's Saturday; you got a bag load of welfare checks and you're three hours late delivering them. Just watch yourself. You get off here and catch that bus, twenty-eight, just sittin' over there. Driver's a nice guy named Burt. He'll get you there and, hopefully, back again."

I thanked him and walked across the street. The bus door was open and as I climbed the steps, I guessed right away that I was in trouble because he was talking to the man behind him who had an Oakland police uniform on and was fitted with a radio and carried a weapon in the holster at his right side and a night stick on the other. He was black as was the driver. From the look on their faces as they stared at me, I saw empathy and pity. "You a student?" the officer asked. I nodded. "You're white," they said in unison.

"That sounds like it's not good."

"It's just uncomfortable. Look, this is a rough place, that's why I ride this bus eight hours a day. But most of the people you'll meet will be nice."

"And the rest?"

"Just watch your back. Also, you got what they need most so I think you'll be okay."

We wound up Fourth Street to my stop. The driver said, "See you in about an hour." I walked across the street. The project was five eight-story buildings with no landscaping and a sand and grass area where the swings looked broken and rusted. I got to the edge of what I guessed was supposed to be a park and turned left into the project. I hadn't gone fifty yards when a mob of at least a hundred Blacks shouting and hooting came towards me from behind the first building.

"Where the hell you been, you white motherfucker!?" They yelled over and over. "Give us our checks, Honkie bastard! You're late as hell. Bet you delivered all the checks to your white customers. Who gives a shit about us?"

I was so overwhelmed that I almost turned and ran. The only reason I didn't was because they'd have caught me. I was scared shitless and almost in tears, but I walked straight through the crowd and saw a dry fountain full of cigarette butts in the middle of the square around which were the buildings. There was a raised low wall into which the water had once poured, and I climbed up on it and put my mail bag between my legs in fear of it being stolen. Then I did something against all federal rules. I took out the checks which were in alphabetical order and started half screaming names. The crowd surrounded me, and their noise quieted. I would call a name, hear someone shout and see them

93

motion. I threw each check in their general direction. By the letter 'C' I was getting into a rhythm and the crowd's hostility seemed to have ebbed.

As the checks went out, the crowd got smaller and I could see that my thrusts went closer. It took me over an hour to pass out the checks. The sun was hot, and my shirt and face were soaked with sweat. When all the checks were done, and the crowd dispersed—they didn't seem to care about the rest of the mail—I set the remaining mail on the fountain wall and walked back out to the bus stop. Nobody bothered me. I had to wait about thirty minutes and the bus driver finally came with his cop escort. They both had a good laugh on me as I climbed on board.

"Glad you made it. We thought when you didn't make it in an hour we'd have to send reinforcements in to get you. Judging from your shirt, you must have had quit a workout." The driver handed me some paper towels and I wiped my face as we pulled away.

"I'll guarantee you both that you won't see me ever again on welfare check day." They laughed. I didn't tell them it wasn't a laughing matter.

I punched out. Haime had already gone home and the place was quiet. I couldn't wait to stand in the shower.

After the shower, I ate a small can of beans with a hot dog and drank a beer. I didn't have long to lay on the couch, but I began to feel half human as I walked to Kasha's.

This time she didn't meet me by the door and I had to ring the bell, which I hope she heard. In a moment she was coming down the stairs. She was almost smiling when she opened the door, as if she had plans other than a reading.

Upstairs, the big Victorian windows facing down on Telegraph were covered with curtains so thin that you could see through them. The living room apparently doubled as the place she did her work, because thrown around the chair and ancient burgundy sofa were a variety of pillows in different sizes, shapes and patterns as if some of her customers preferred sitting on the floor. Kasha motioned me towards the couch and lit incense, then turned on a machine that made a low hum before she took a seat on an even older heavily upholstered rocker, also in burgundy. She was dressed as she'd been that morning.

"Okay, so why did you think I needed a reading... if that's what it's called? The room was slightly dark, and she lit a table lamp on the desk next to her chair.

"I can sense such things. I know that you dropped out of school and joined the draft. I know you had some difficulty there and were discharged. I know you've decided to come back to school but don't know why and are really only passing time. I also know you have a beautiful girlfriend and you can't figure out what your relationship is, though you feel close to her but down deep have doubts that she feels the same. That is what I sense."

"I'm sold. How long is a session?"

"Almost an hour, why?"

"I need to call that girl and tell her to come a half hour later for dinner." She pointed at the phone and I called Kim. Luckily, she was in and said fine. I turned back to Kasha. "Well, how—how does this work?"

"I give you a student discount of $50.00 starting with the second visit. I am able to be in touch with the spiritual side of your life, specifically your spiritual guides— forms of energy not humans—and you ask questions and I tell you their answers. Or, I tell you what I may be picking up from them. That's what I'm going to be doing now, thoughts from the spiritual world that have come to me about you, just like what I've told you. You can stop me to ask a question if you need to." She sat up very straight with her hands folded in her lap. Her breath was measured.

"Now your postal job seems like good luck, but a time will come when it takes on more importance."

I was about to ask how the job would become important, but she raised one hand to stop me and said, "Some questions cannot be answered now."

"There is a girl you will become very close with, but she has many troubles."

I assumed she meant Kim but the "many troubles" part didn't seem like Kim. I was afraid to ask.

"Your spiritual guides are pointing someone out, but she is a great distance away, so I can't really make out her face. I don't know who she is or where she fits into your life and the guides only shake their heads when I ask them. The far future is dark. I can't go any further now. Do you have any questions to ask?"

"Yeah. What about school and my studio?"

"You wanted to take six units over next summer, but you won't be able to.

"Why not, I was counting on that?"

The hand up again. After a pause, "No answer now."

"And?"

"No change on the studio until you decide to leave. You're doing well in school, even if you don't know why you're there. You'll learn the way."

"What do you mean, 'the way'?"

"That's up to you, the guides say."

It was becoming frustrating. "I don't get it. Up to me, what?" Kisha opened her eyes and stared at the floor, then closed them again.

"No answer yet." She opened them again. "Anything else?" I didn't know what to say except I was confused. She waited patiently, but all I could manage was a half-perplexed laugh. "Now I'm going to speak with your spiritual guides. Please be still and quiet until I am through."

She closed her eyes and rested against the rocker, slowly making it rock. "I see you under a stone at this moment. Not a cloud because that's too light. It's a big, big rock…. the size of all the islands that make up Japan, an archipelago, and it stretches from now back to before you were born. You have always been able to move under it but it's very hard, like moving through a kind of transparent mud. You don't know it's there nor can you feel it. But, trust me, it is real. You came under it when you were born. It seems endless, but you can end it, you can make it vanish. There is sky above it: clear, bright."

"I don't understand. What is it? Why is it there?"

"Wait," she interrupted. "Don't interrupt until I'm finished. There's not much more. You have the power but you're weak, which is what you should be since it's nearly impossible to take an action against what is unconscious. I asked the guides, but they aren't talking, that energy isn't moving. I'm through now. Look, before you speak. I don't understand what it is or why it's there."

"But can't you give me any help?" I felt like I was in a Kafka trial, on the stand for a crime but not knowing why or how to defend myself or how to find out. She scared me.

chapter thirteen

Kasha had really knocked me out with her reading. I sat on the couch waiting for Kim and was beginning to believe it. There were several revelations I was turning over in my mind. There was the idea about the troubled girlfriend, how my PO job would become more important, and what was this rock I had always lived with and under? If she couldn't make any sense out of this or find me the way towards a solution, then what was I supposed to do—a guy who had no alleged access to the energy fields that Kasha did? I almost ran to the door as I heard Kim coming up the stairs.

"Hi." She gave me a long embrace right in the door entry. I could feel the firmness of her breasts and our bodies pressing against each other as I pulled her, almost anxiously, to me. We were kissing all over each other's face and mouth and I wondered what had set us off. "Can we make love first and then I'll tell you about the reading?"

She put her arms quickly around my neck and grinned. "You need permission?"

I carried her to the couch and we frantically pulled it out and undressed ourselves. We were both naked when we fell onto the quilt. There was such a hunger for sexual release that it couldn't have been more than five minutes before we both climaxed and lay still, my leg gently across her body. "How did that happen?" I laughed easily.

Kim shook her head and her face held a puzzled look. Her lips just kept smiling and it came to me that I wanted to marry her. To support her. To share a real love with children, a real love of family with her. I was nuts. I lay down and looked at the ceiling with half closed eyes. Sunlight from the hardwood reflected in large sun shadows against it.

"You were going to tell me about the reading before we were so rudely interrupted." Her laugh was truly joyous, as if she'd beaten me in saying something we both were thinking.

"Does she drive you wild like that? I don't think you should have any more sessions with her," Kim teased.

"No, she didn't show me that side of herself, if there really is such a thing. And, yes, I would like to tell you about it though what we just did was far better."

Kim rose from the quilt and kissed my cheek. "It is only us. That makes me happy." She crawled under the quilt and propped herself up on a pillow. "Okay, I'm ready for your adventure."

I got into the other side and did the same, turning so I could see her face. "It was more a question session with not many answers, I'm afraid. It scared me the way she could read my past and future. She said I had always lived under a rock the size of all the islands of Japan. Like I've been wading through transparent mud all my life and not being conscious of it. She also said that a girl was or would be, I can't remember which, in my life who had lots of troubles. Finally, my PO job would become of great importance to me. But the kicker was that she couldn't explain what any of these meant. Said, the energy wasn't flowing… whatever that means. Can you understand any of it?"

Kim looked up at the late sun shadows for a minute before she spoke. "I didn't tell you, but I went to her in my freshman year to ask about what sorority to join. I'd been rushed by four of them. She wasn't abstract like she was with you. Told me straight out which was best for me and why. Now that I remember that I realize she was wrong, but I've been stuck where I chose. Yet I think your situation was different and more of a question of life-changing things, especially the rock and the girl with troubles. Did you think the latter was me?"

"No way. I've never seen you as someone with lots of troubles. I can see it with your parent's situation but that's all. But I don't know any girl with troubles…. and I don't want to."

"You never know, though."

"What do you mean?

"Things do change, Mark."

"Is that a hint, after the closeness of us for the last half hour?"

"I'm off to law school and you're still here. How are we going to adjust to that?"

"I think we can, if we want to"

"I think the rock part is pretty up front. It's the heaviest form of darkness, don't you think? Isn't that really what you've lived under?"

"But she couldn't say how I get out from under it: get out from the need to be punished, to fail."

"She must have said you'd have to figure that out, didn't she? That's pretty much what she told me about the sorority choice."

"Except I don't have anything to start with."

"Sure, you do. The rock as big as all the Japanese islands."

"Thanks a lot, that's a big help."

"I don't know about the PO or the girl with troubles, unless I'm suddenly going to have them."

I tweaked her nose and she playfully pushed my arm away. "I wish I could help with your parent's situation. I don't think I really had parents"

"I'm tired of thinking and talking about it. Let's drive over to the city and let it distract us from all this stuff for a while. Are you game for that? I know a place in North Beach that serves the best hamburgers, fries and malts."

"I just don't want to get involved in the whole North Beach scene. Is that okay?"

"When did I ever try to do that?" She asked.

She was right. Kim was even more conservative than me when it came to the ruckus of North Beach. We got there in very early twilight, so the crowds and the rest were minimal. She was right also about the hamburgers, malts and fries at a tiny place called "Little Joe's" on Columbus just off Broadway. She told me that Joe owned the building and it had been in the family for several generations. If it hadn't, it would have long ago been swallowed by bigness, even with local patronage. It only had about fifteen stools and the hamburger was such high quality that it was served without condiments on a special French roll baked fresh that day. They also had malts with real ice cream, so we needed some walking around time after the meal. We spent about an hour in City Lights bookstore where I found more works by this poet, Gary Snyder, who wrote *Riprap*. The guy at the cash register told me that besides being a poet and world traveler, he was also an organic farmer who practiced Zen and lived near a little town that had become a major sixties retreat north of San Francisco and inland.

On the drive home, I told Kim about the book and its author.

"But how do you make a living if you just write poetry, travel and farm?"

"I'd like to find out." I realized then that it was the poet's lifestyle that really had attracted me but I, like Kim, also wondered how you could live that free and support yourself in this world.

When she stopped in front of my place, she took my hand as if we were about to part forever which was in sharp contrast to earlier that day.

"Promise you won't be insulted by what I'm about to say?"

"Okay, I promise, even though I don't know what it is."

"It's this." She looked all around the car, but I couldn't figure what she meant.

"Can you be more specific?"

"The Volvo."

"What about it?"

"They're buying me a new car to start school. I know this one isn't so pretty and could use a paint job and has 100,000 miles on it, but—and here's where I don't want you to be insulted—I want you to have it if you want it."

She just about knocked me over. "Sure, that would be incredible." I leaned over and gave her a huge kiss. "That's no insult at all."

"Is six hundred too much? You could pay it off a little every month and you'd have wheels."

"That's too generous. I'm poor but I could pay more."

"No, I talked to my Dad and he okayed it. Of course, always the lawyer, he wanted you to sign a contract."

"I will."

"No." We kissed again.

"I really appreciate this. Maybe someday it'll be our car."

"I would hope by then we could afford better. Here's an idea. Let's take a drive up to the Russian River in the next couple of weeks. Maybe one day, maybe stay over. We could stop in Jenner. I've never been there but I hear the restaurants are mostly family style and terrific. Sneak down to the river at a property where no one's home. Christen the car. It would be just a week or so before finals. What do you say? We could even sleep in the car if we stay over. Save some bucks."

"I like all of that except the sleep over." She laughed.

chapter fourteen

When May rolled around, graduation was close for Kim and I sensed a tension in her and myself, but I couldn't explain it except for the obvious: she was moving back to L.A. I had been offered an early final exam choice in Anthropology and I took it and pulled an "A." As for the lit class in Modern American authors, I wrote a final paper early which was an analysis of *Riprap* and *Cold Mountain Poems* including all I could find, mostly from avant-garde magazines on the author, Gary Snyder. I was taking the same teacher who had given me a "D" last semester, and it was a good feeling when she told me I had chosen a non-mainstream writer—the only one who did—and beautifully integrated his story with the book. Another "A." So, I had nothing really left to do but study for Sociology and had plenty of time to ace that.

I liked the Lit class best because it was only twelve students compared to the others which were two hundred and three hundred-fifty, the latter two being more the norm in a university this size. The twelve could hardly be called unique, but there were a few students who were not afraid to give their thoughts and ideas regularly. One of them was very unique, at least to me. She was a junior. She wore nothing but high collar Hindu colorful shirts, jeans and—always—thong sandals. It was hard not to notice she had a

great body, almost as firm as an athlete. The Hindu shirts
were loose, but every time she stretched you could tell. And
there was no denying that when she wore Levi's or short
shorts, she had a very firm butt. I guess she would be
classified as full of mood swings, because some days she'd
be grumpy and some elated. I got the impression that she
was on something, but then she'd snap out of it and be
normal.

Besides the great body, she had truly unique features
and hair. Her skin was almost ghostly white. It was the kind
of skin that only burns and never tans. She confided in me
once as we were leaving class that it was the single most
frustrating thing because she loved the sun and being
outdoors. She had sort of full lips with lipstick that was a
combination between orange and red, very bright. Her
cheekbones were almost too high, and she had eyes that were
the weirdest color—a medium gray. She also had this
sensuality in the way she moved her arms and mouth. The
muscles in her arms actually responded, flexed, when she
made a point, and that would be followed by the pursing of
her lips like she was trying to kiss the air. The most striking
feature about her was her hair. It was white blonde and she'd
had it put into cornrows which gave the impression that she
was always standing in a high wind.

Anyway, I don't know what got me off on her.
Taylor was her name and she was majoring in math but

wanted to be a poet and she'd read a lot of Snyder and read my paper after I got it back. She loved it. So, away from this diversion and back to a different reality with Kim. I called her, and she accepted a one-day excursion to the Russian River and Jenner.

We got to Jenner about 1:30 pm. The little town looked right off a movie set: quiet, moderate traffic and surprisingly few people for a Saturday because the winter eliminated the crush of summer tourists, mostly from the bay area.

We found what looked like a locals' pub and sat in back by a garden with a glass of beer. We split a cob salad which turned out to be delicious, accompanied by a small loaf of French bread baked fresh from the pub's kitchen. It was a perfect late May afternoon with a light breeze and a sun that was warm but not hot. Afterward, we walked around town visiting the local shops. We didn't buy anything, except Kim somehow found a set of fuzzy dice to hang over the bar of my rearview mirror as a christening present for my Volvo. I couldn't believe they even had something that tacky in a town more famous for its art.

After a couple hours, we walked over to the river which flowed dark in the shadow of all the trees that grew along its banks. It had been a bad year for snow, so the current ran more shallow than usual. We found the public access area but even in winter it was too crowded for us, so we got back in the car and started down the road below town, lined with cottages and cabins that fronted the river. We found a small, older cottage with no garage, no car and all the curtains closed which had to be a signal to us or burglars that the place was closed. We figured no one would come that late in the afternoon and pulled into a spot off the edge of the pebble driveway. There was a long distance between the house and the next one and it was thick with shrubs and a dense forest of oaks, eucalyptus and cedar blocking any view of us from the next house.

We lay out a blanket with a couple of old pillows Kim had, and settled into the warmth and shadows that fell upon us. The sky was glassy blue and all you could hear was the peaceful and quiet movement of the river. Kim said she didn't feel it, but after a while I felt this deep silence that permeated everything: the river, the leaves, the grass and sun. I'd never felt anything like it and I couldn't figure out where it came from. I probably could have sat in it for an hour, but then Kim rose up on one elbow and gently stroked my outstretched arm which felt so erotic. I rolled towards her and she lay back against the blanket, grabbed my head and began gently kissing me nonstop all over my face and neck. She wore a sundress, so her shoulders were bare and exposed to light falling on them through the spaces between the leaves. We kissed and licked each other, almost biting in our excitement.

Kim looked up at me and smiled. She whispered, "You know I'm a nice sorority girl, but I want you to forget that and screw me!" She pulled down the sundress and got her panties off before I could hardly unbutton my shirt. In fact, I had a hell of a time undressing the rest of me because she kept pulling me down on her. Soon we were both unclothed enough to let our bodies touch and she virtually pulled me into her and the rocking motion of our bodies took over. I was flat out surprised that I could last that long with that many raw sensations banging at me, but I did and when it ended we lay as one until my weight on her stomach and my aching arms forced me to roll off into a collapse on the blanket. We must have laid there caressing each other for an hour, and as I was coming out of that—our biggest euphoria ever—I couldn't keep being worried out of my mind. I worried about getting her pregnant, although she took the pill and we had always used a condom, and about the owners of the property showing up. It was almost like I couldn't just relax into it, just enjoy such a rare moment.

So, we got up and dressed, hugged, folded the blanket and walked slowly in the late sun to the Volvo. As we drove back toward town, she combed her hair and mine and we looked pretty presentable when we got out about 5:00 and went into the Italian restaurant Dave and Annie insisted we try. It was big and family style, but uncrowded since we'd come so early. We ordered a bottle of the wine recommended by the waitress for the kind of food we ordered. We were alone by a window. When it came, we toasted twice and drank twice. "It may not be expensive but, damn, it is good."

"To a moment in heaven."

"Thank you, Kim."

"And you." We toasted a third time. "And now we're going to leave this all behind." She took my hands in hers.

"No recriminations, Mark. Let's ride this out and see where it goes."

"I could transfer to UCLA and get my job at the PO down there, it's nationwide."

"It's too impractical."

I nodded and had to admit it. But that didn't make it any better.

We hardly spoke, driving home. I let her off and we exchanged kisses in the silence.

chapter fifteen

Two weeks later exams were over. I was taking Kim to the airport the next evening. We were spending the last day having a picnic. We had hardly seen each other during exam week, and the next night would be our last for a time. The negative me thought, 'perhaps forever.' I couldn't accept that.

Kim had an eight o'clock flight and we arrived at seven because she said she was always nervous about not catching a flight, just like me. We both wanted to talk, so we sat in the terminal on a bench covered with blue leather and riddled with creases. It reminded me of the L.A. bus terminal bench a long time ago.

I got us coffee and had to fight through the crowd streaming out. I realized then that Friday nights were the busiest time since many were returning from a week away on business along with early tourists heading into the city. When I finally got back, I handed her the coffee and remarked, "Have you ever noticed the faces and the body types? They both leap out at me."

"Meaning?"

"Faces neutral. Body types fat and getting fatter."

She smiled and motioned me to sit. Then she kissed me, which I wished she hadn't done.

"You've been in a college town too long, Mark. Everybody's young and mostly trim." She motioned with her hand. "This is the real world, isn't it?"

"I hope not."

"Well, it is. I've watched people in my Dad's firm. The same thing happens, and they're probably making a lot more money that this crowd. Especially the women. They arrive as young attorneys, looking fit and in two or three years many of them have gained twenty pounds and are dropping aspirin or valium at the water cooler a few times a day."

"I hope that's not going to be you."

This time she laughed. "What, don't you want a bit of plumpness?"

I just grinned. "Being the bosses' daughter, that won't happen to you."

"I still have to compete to be hired after law school, though I'll have an advantage being able to intern every summer. And maybe I won't be smart enough."

"I've always imagined you teaching somewhere like Big Sur and running psychology sessions at Esalen on the side for extra money and me maybe in the forest service there. Like Gary Snyder in *Riprap*."

She paused for a minute to look at the crowd as it was slowly thinning out. Then suddenly she was holding my hands and looking me straight in the eye. "We're doing everything to avoid us."

"Yeah, I know. But you're off to be a big-time lawyer and I don't know what I'm off to be, and we're looking at your years still in school, and mine. And you say it's too impractical for me to come south."

Kim kept holding my hands gently. I felt like dragging her back to Berkeley.

"If it's supposed to last, then we'll make it happen somehow: letters, short visits, whatever."

"I know. I hope. It's quarter to eight, we better get you boarded." I pulled her up with me and grabbed her luggage. We held each other until she became the last person to board. She turned and blew me a kiss, then rounded the corner and disappeared. The boarding area was empty, and the airline employees had gone when I went back into the aisle.

I started to walk. There were very few people, and I stopped a janitor to ask why. She said there were no more flights from that terminal until eleven, and that's why she was cleaning. When I reached the bench we'd sat on, I stared at the cracked blue leather for a moment before sitting down again. It suddenly got quiet, with just a few people passing and the janitor pushing a cart whose wheels sounded like rubber being dragged across the floor.

I kept looking towards Kim's terminal and felt stuck on the bench.

"nothing is left but the weight
the nostalgia for the weight of a living existence"

The Seferis poem wouldn't leave me. I was finally beginning to understand the meaning of those two lines. I felt the bench. At least it wasn't greasy like the bus terminal one. I felt honestly alone, a feeling I couldn't even remember from my prison days. Letters, short visits, whatever, I thought.

I didn't remember getting up and then I was in the early summer darkness staring at the fuzzy dice on the rear-view mirror.

<hr />

I didn't realize the impact Kim's leaving would have on me. I was thinking about us all the time. Just like my imagined parents, I retreated into her—my imagined lover. I kept trying to develop a scenario of an imagined life with her. I was used to punishment, to failure, and I kept imagining that was where I was. I had failed because I couldn't offer her anything worth staying for; I was still lost in ideas and I couldn't figure how these fit together. Now I was punishing myself with nostalgia, with the weight of our existence together. All of us moving through the living experience were only nostalgia because we were moving, impermanent.

With the coming of summer, I spent a lot more time in bed. There was nothing to do, and nowhere I thought I wanted to go. All I had to do was the PO in the afternoon. I had extended my hours purposely, so I wasn't getting home until ten or eleven. The money was good, but I knew the deeper reason was filling up hours that had opened without Kim. After some weeks of that, I called Dave and he and Annie invited me over for dinner. We hadn't seen each other since before finals.

Somewhere I read that people who lived together or are married looked much alike. That was Annie and Dave. They both had light brown hair and eyes, round faces—his more than hers—medium lips, perfect white teeth and clear skin. From a distance, if their backs were toward you, they looked a lot alike except her hair was thick and closely cut and his was long, thin and beginning to go. They'd met at a dance on a blind date at her fancy prep school and were still together. Both families had money. Annie's was old, and Dave's father had made his creating a real estate empire. I know they weren't sweating incomes the way so many grads were doing.

I hadn't met Annie until Berkeley but had known Dave since junior high and we'd been close friends ever since. I could always share my thoughts with him, and she was the same way. They used their high, wide front porch as the location for outdoor activities since their backyard was at too much of an incline. The residential traffic was light up where they lived so the porch was private. Dave was just stoking the barbeque when I drove up the hill and parked in the driveway.

He waved. "Hey, nice car. I'll grab you a beer." He disappeared inside. From the plate on the shelf to the side of the grill it looked like my favorite summer meal. The plate had both beautifully formed organic hamburgers and organic hot dogs. That had to mean Annie had made her famous and terrific potato salad and fresh corn on the cob that was wrapped in foil and wedged next to the plate. I recalled that as a kid, my Mother never used my Dad's barbeque. After he died, it sat and eventually was given away.

"Your summer going okay?" He handed me a bottle of the German beer they drank at barbeques.

"Thanks. Yeah, except for I'm sure you know what."

"Annie and Kim grabbed an hour on the phone this morning. How's the car?"

"Terrific."

"At least that's good."

"And she misses you horribly already," Annie said, coming out the screened front door with a plate of cheese and crackers. I looked doubtful I guess. "Marco, don't you look like that. She even started to cry."

Annie offered me some Brie on a cracker. "Then why did she have to go?"

"Don't you think the more honest question is 'What reason would she stay except the two of you in some small apartment, maybe even in Oakland, and her working full time at some dumb job to help make ends meet?"

Dave interrupted her. "Come on, Annie, that's below the belt, don't you think?"

"Thanks Dave, but no, I hate to admit Annie's point. In fact, it angers the hell out of me, mainly because I set myself up for failure when I let my grades drop and left school and for no reason except that there was nothing I felt even halfway passionate about. I'd have graduated with you guys.

"I'm sorry Marco, I didn't mean to be hard on you. I can only tell you what she said."

"That's no sweat but it does raise this awful long-time question of why Kim and I find ourselves in this position? It's again this pretty much unconscious failure syndrome that's plagued me, without me seeing it, all my life."

Dave was loading the grill with all the ingredients. "But I don't think it's a failure. You heard what Annie said. Kim was crying. That has to mean she's missing you too."

"Yeah, I can see that but why couldn't we just stop where we were? Why couldn't we just start here? I know money would be tight for a long time, but eventually that would even out."

"That means different things to different people."
Annie adjusted the corn on the grill. "Dave and I are
incredibly lucky. We know that. Money isn't our worry but
trying to find a place to contribute now that we're out of
school is a whole different ball game. It's tempting to head
up to Mendocino, buy a place on some acres, smoke a lot of
dope, maybe write or paint or whatever, and avoid the whole
issue of finding a place. Heck, Dave and I have been asking
that question since we came here."

"But there are people who've dropped out who
didn't have money. Look at this guy, Snyder, whose book I
told you about." I drank some beer and ate more cheese and
crackers. "He has worked his way around the world on
tankers, spent time in Japanese monasteries, worked in the
forest up north. And there must be others. Kim could get her
teaching credential while I finish the BA and then we could
go someplace away from all the shit were exposed to every
day. I could work in the forest too."

Annie came and sat down on the porch steps with
me. "Kim gave up long ago on the idea of some low paying
job teaching English in high school. I know she told you she
was thinking about it but, honestly, Kim sometimes bends
another person's way because she doesn't want to offend
them. And her Dad has been on her since high school to go
to law school. She worked in his office for two summers

when she was at school. He went to USC for law too. You can see the pattern?"

"Why can't it be broken?"

"It could be but imagine the pressure she's under?"

"Whatever happened to the idea that a kid should try to find his or her dream and follow it? The sixties and all that stuff?"

"Marco, you know that's just the old American illusion. It probably was only real over a hundred year ago when gold was discovered here. And even then, the dream was more a nightmare for most of those who tried." Dave was flipping the burgers and dogs.

"Well, I'm not...."

Annie interrupted. She squeezed my arm. "That's why she's so torn, so mixed up. She has feelings for you. But the dream she may want is buried by the expectations of her family. You're gonna have to face it, Marco. Maybe she will hate law school or being a lawyer. Maybe you two will get back together. Come on, let's eat."

We sat until the summer darkness fell over the porch, spending most of our time talking about Kim and my separation. But no satisfactory answers came of it.

They took a whole month driving to Canada along the Pacific and I kept stacking up the hours and some savings from my PO job. I only heard once by phone from Kim and two weeks later I got this long and beautiful goodbye letter. I'd never felt like giving up before. This was the first time.

chapter sixteen

It rained in August, more rain than the Bay Area could remember. I had to buy another set of rubber boots, but they were worth it. I stopped as usual at the Mediterranean café and decided to read a few pages from *Zen and the Art of Motorcycle Maintenance* which I'd already read twice and still was finding it too deep for me. I wrote a note to Dino asking him about it. He hadn't left for Africa yet. He summed up the whole father-son relationship which I got and the idea of the guy finally coming to terms with the world that he had lost a sane relationship with. But it was the deeper philosophical stuff I just wasn't getting, the stuff driving him nuts yet freeing him. I'd only re-read two pages when someone tapped me on the shoulder.

I turned and looked up and saw that weird haircut, white-blonde set in cornrows. It was the girl from my English Lit class last semester when I dropped out. "Mind if I join you?" she said, not waiting for an answer. She set her tiny espresso cup down, leaned over and banged my knuckles, using the latest hip handshake. "Taylor Alway, from English Lit 200, remember? Call me Lor, it's shorter and easier. You're a mailman in your spare time?" I was just coming off some dense writing in *Motorcycle Maintenance* and I looked a little puzzled. I must have stared at her for at least a minute. Next to an Albino, she had the whitest and

smoothest skin, completely without blemishes. What I
noticed most was a muscular neck, a strong chin, real blonde
eyebrows and lashes, and thin lips. All of her face, without
make-up. She had arms with the "cut" —kind of like a
weightlifter yet feminine, and her shoulders looked strong as
the tank top exposed them. We had both participated a lot in
class, but never got around to names or after class
conversation.

"Lor, it's Mark Eliot. Yeah, I remember you from
the class, you and I seemed to talk the most. Nice to meet
you."

She sipped the espresso. Her lips seemed to fold
over the small cup as she did. "Better watch that 'nice to
meet you,' it may not be." She laughed as if she'd said
something funnier than what she'd said. Then suddenly, she
thumbed her nose at a guy who had just walked in, and he
thumbed her back.

"Who's that?"

"Kind of an ex but nothing serious. He's pretty
much a jerk but a legend in his own mind." She laughed that
big laugh again and stuck a couple of sticks of Juicy Fruit
gum in her mouth. "You live up near Sather, don't you?" I
nodded. "I thought I'd seen you turn up there sometimes
when I came off campus. What'd you do time in military
prison for?"

She was getting a little too personal now. "Who told you that?"

"Nobody. I work in the Housing Office and I read the files that sound interesting. Yours was."

"I thought those were treated as confidential."

"What really is confidential, anything?"

"I guess not from what you're saying." I think I sounded a little irritated.

"I'm sorry. I promise I won't tell anyone." The lips made a large smile. It suddenly made her friendlier. Lor spit the wad of gum into her empty espresso cup and set it down.

"Want some espresso gum?" She pushed the cup toward me with a straight face and it was impossible not to laugh at her outlandishness.

Out of nowhere she asked, "Want some dinner? We're great cooks where I live."

At that moment, I didn't know what to make of Taylor. She had said some crazy things in class, both about the books we read and politics in general, but this was a side of her I'd never seen. Everything she'd said I thought was intelligent. She was at once assuming and unassuming. And weird. "Wha...when?"

"Tonight, around seven. I live up Dwight to the second street then right to number 98. It's a green and yellow Victorian with a huge front porch and red mailbox."

"I know the place. You're on my Saturday delivery route. I'm heading up that way now."

"Any mail for me?"

"It's a federal offense if I give it to you. If I do I lose my job."

"Don't do that then."

"I won't, and sure I'll be there around six-thirty."

chapter seventeen

I decided to take out a no-show route after I finished mine, so I didn't get through until almost 3:30 because it was up in the hills and I'd never worked it before. From the first time, Haime knew I wouldn't take Hunter's Point again and never tried to give it to me. But in return I was glad to pick up the overtime on other no-show routes. Since Kim had left, I was building up a decent savings account.

I decided to walk over to Lor's rather than drive. It gave me some time to try and figure out what I was getting into. My impression of her in class and now hadn't changed. I thought she was the strangest of the strange, but I had the feeling that her wiseass attitude was covering something. She was brass in school, but almost always retreated when someone challenged her point of view, even when I thought it was right and perceptive.

The house looked newly painted and the windows appeared clean, but walking to the front porch I saw that the lawn needed water and cutting and had grown up about two feet. Lor was sitting in an old swing on the porch with a guy whose beard and black hair looked about as neglected as the lawn.

"Charlie here," she pointed a thumb at the guy next to her, "is supposed to cut the grass but he just got back from a five-day hunger strike for a guy on death row up at the San Quentin." Charlie looked too young to me set of

on a hunger strike. He smiled and waved. "Is vegetarian stew and French bread okay with you? It's in the oven right now. Freshly baked peach pie and vanilla ice cream for dessert." She opened a large freezer container on a low table next to the swing and offered me a beer. "You want a drag?" She took the joint from Charlie and pushed it towards me.

I waved my hand as casually as I could. "Beer's fine for now."

She seemed to spring off the swing. Lor grabbed my arm. "Come on, you can keep me company in the kitchen. Eddy, Georgia and Phil should be downstairs for supper pretty soon." I sat on a stool and watched her putter around the large kitchen. It was hot in there with the oven on and her super white skin that was exposed, including her face, were flush from it. I almost felt like putting a wet towel against her forehead, but she was moving around so much it would have been hard to get her to settle down long enough for that.

I caught myself thinking that she had a certain sexiness about her. It was nothing like Kim, and she seemed way too wild to me but I couldn't put the sex aside. Her smoking dope and what else (?) was something I didn't want to get involved with, but I had to admit that she had this lure about her that touched on a kind of sweetness though I assumed that she was anything but innocent. I was pulled from my thoughts when she rang a ship's bell by the cupboard and threw me another beer from the refrigerator which I almost dropped.

I assumed we were going to have dinner when I helped her carry the food to a huge dining room table that must have come with the house and had seen better days. By now Eddy, Georgia, Phil and Charlie were already seated. They all followed some guru I'd never heard of, and part of that discipline was to eat in silence. Apparently, the guru drank cheap wine because it was abundant in large jugs of either white or red. I was surprised that Lor, given what I saw as her kind of off-the-wall personality, was a really good cook because I had never liked vegetarian cooking, and this tasted fine.

When we finished, it was like a flood gate had been opened because it seemed like everybody was talking at once except myself and Lor, who I thought would be jumping into the thick of it. She was listening with her white-blonde head tilted slightly to the side and her glass of wine touching her lips but not drinking any. Finally Eddy and Charlie looked over at me as if I had just appeared from nowhere.

"Hey, Mark, what do you think of all this?"

"I don't know. The way you all were going at it I couldn't make heads or tails out of the conversation. What was the subject?" They paused a moment and then laughed. Lor kind of tickled me under the arm and pushed me at the same time as she joined in.

Georgia had a cross tattooed just above her breasts. She wore a small jade stone necklace and a blue linen dress that reached down to her bare feet. "Don't mind these guys, Mark. They're all pretty nutso!"

"Yeah, I gathered that" I laughed. "So, what was the subject?"

"Civil Rights" Phil said and looked at the others. "I think."

"Right on!" Charlie extend his arm and hand into a Black Power salute.

"Well, I honestly don't know civil rights from the man in the moon. I'm ignorant. Somehow it all just passed me by. Though I did know a black guy in the military who I got friendly with since we were cellmates in prison. He was the first black person I've ever known, and he thought the civil rights thing was mostly bullshit because nothing has or is going to change from his view."

They all started to talk at once until Georgia got the floor. "How can your friend say that? We've got Title VII against discrimination and a half a dozen laws that are critical to stopping prejudice."

"I'm only saying, 'from his view' and he's just one person. Maybe he's wrong. I don't know, Georgia. But he offered a lot of proof, and it sure blew my mind."

"Like what?" Charlie asked.

I was about to answer when Lor sat up straight in her chair and interrupted, a re-occurring characteristic I was beginning to see. "Jeez guys, do all our conversations have to be intense?" She got up and started clearing the table with Georgia's and Phil's help. We all pitched in to wash and dry and then took our dessert into the massive living room and its ancient, worn and overstuffed couches and chairs. It was raining again and cold for August, so Charlie touched off the fire in the enormous field stone hearth. We sat around somewhat groggy after the meal. Someone rolled and lit a joint, I think it was Georgia, and it went around as we sat in silence listening to the rain on the porch steps.

I faked a few puffs but was afraid to really inhale because of the experience I'd had at the end of high school. It was just before summer and my closest friend in school had gotten hold of some hash and we were sharing it in his car in the school parking lot. It was the first time for me and he compassionately instructed me without making fun of my lack of experience. We were between study hall and lunch and I didn't feel much from my prolonged and amateur inhalations until we got out and went in to lunch. I suddenly felt like I was seeing the world different and had lost control, which scared me more. By the time I got home, I had to lay on the bed and when I closed my eyes, I felt like I was falling through a black void. Through the liquid darkness I saw a policeman and frantically reached out, but it was as if he didn't see me and I kept falling. I staggered, sweating, into the shower and somehow the warm water bought me slowly back to a sort of normal. My Grandmother was taking a nap in her room and I snuck into my Mother's room and closed the door, quietly calling my friend to ask him about what had happened. He just said it happened that way to some people but most just get mellow. I hung up feeling anything but mellow, and that night I fell exhausted to sleep. When I awoke, the feelings and vision were gone but the fear of it reoccurring lingered most of the summer in the back of my mind.

About ten, I got up to go and Lor escorted me to the front porch. The others didn't move, they seemed to be gently drifting out in space. I was about to say 'goodnight' when she suddenly grabbed my left arm and began stroking it. "It's okay if you don't do weed." She had the sweetest smile, as if protecting me from something I feared. I smiled back.

"Thanks, it's just me. You're a good cook."

As suddenly she dropped my arm and said, "See you around," and turned back toward the front door. The rain had stopped. I looked back, but she was already inside the house.

I couldn't figure her out, but the word 'unique' came to mind for no reason I could understand. Maybe *too* unique.

She kept reappearing in my mind as the week went by. I bought my books for the semester and worked sorting at the PO. I could graduate next May if I took a full load, which I didn't. I spent a lot of my free time not reading required material but from the books Dino had given to me. I had gotten as far as I could go with the first two and was focusing on Wendell Berry's *The Unsettling of America*. I'd really only gotten interested in reading during my first year at the university, so I was slow and wasn't understanding as much as I'd liked to. But I thought I understood the essence of his work, which was that the further removed from the land we became, the more insane our society would become. I wasn't sure and read it again, but I couldn't get much beyond the general theme. What I did feel, as I had with the other works, was that the authors were truly individuals of integrity and had deep concerns they weren't afraid to voice; something that was new to me.

I understood a little about integrity because my Mother had it. I remember her crying at dinner because she had refused to reduce her two-week trips to New York to one week. She had argued that it wasn't enough time to do her work properly, but the new merchandise manager said one week was the new policy for budget purposes. My mother had only three months to retirement and my Grandmother said to do as she was told, or it might jeopardize that. But my Mother instead had gone to the president of the store to plead her case and he had returned her to the two-week policy. I realized just recently that she had not been afraid to stand up for what she believed. I had just begun to read Howard Zinn's *Passionate Declarations* and from the first chapter, I realized that America had two faces; one was what we said we were and the other was what we in truth actually were. I could not believe we didn't do what we said. I didn't want to believe Zinn. I wish she could have given love beside integrity.

chapter eighteen

I reread Kim's good-bye letter for the millionth time.

Dear Mark,

I realize that there is no way to say this, but I'll try. I have enjoyed this semester with you and I know you have too. But I think it's time we faced where our paths are going. I'm afraid our paths are separating now, and I can't see any way to bring them together again and I have honestly thought about it. I will be in law school and you still have at least a semester and maybe summer session before you finish, and so much can happen in that time. As much as it hurts to say it, I think our paths will always be separate because at your own admission you aren't sure what you want. I don't know what you want either. I don't know what I want, but I grew up in an environment surrounded by a certain kind of person. And you did the same. I've gone over this a lot with my parents, and they insist that you and I just happened at the wrong time. I'm sorry, but I understand what they are saying. I hope you won't hate me and will think of all the beautiful moments we had, as I will.

Love and Blessings, Kim

I took a swig of beer at my desk and stared out at another overcast day. She was classy to the end and I appreciated that, but it didn't make it any easier realizing that we'd probably never see each other again. I walked to north campus and up to the park in the lower hills. The weather had kept everyone away, and I sat on a rock by the duck pond to avoid the still wet grass. I wanted to be a duck.

They looked so unencumbered. I thought of all the things about Kim that she had now taken from my life and knew that she had cared—actually *cared*—for me. But had I cared for her? Did I know how? During our time, there had been no strings attached to our relationship, no judgements, no social restraints. I started to cry softly and did for some time. The ducks didn't seem to mind.

I had been working almost forty hours a week between an extra route Saturday and full shifts during the week. I sent a note to Kim with the rest of the Volvo payment. I still had a good chunk left over. It meant I'd met all my expenses up through summer with my savings and my regular hours during school. I never said anything in my note to Kim except 'Thank you' as I'm sure she didn't want to get a back and forth thing going. And God bless my landlord. He knocked off a hundred a month for me to clean the steps and front entry every week.

I've finished the Zinn book on history and am reading it twice because I think so much the way he does, but never realized it until reading him. It's a mystery to me how I came to think that way, because all of my "family" is very conservative and business-oriented as opposed to people-oriented. I'd love to be able to talk this book over with Kim or Dino. It's frustrating not having someone to drop down to coffee with and talk about it, but who knows who I will might meet this semester?

This week the plaza is crowded again since school has started. I like the sound of most of my classes and am happy to be finished with any kind of science: I've just never been able to grasp it. All the classes are gigantic but we have small TA sessions each week so that should help. These big sections make me look at education differently than when I began. There's been a lot of talk and press this past ten years that education has become nothing but the extension of the factory or corporation, and its only purpose is to find a good paying job defined as "a career." It looks like if I stay on track, I should have my BA in English the end of the summer. Hopefully, I will have been able to bring my grade point to within a respectable range by then in case I decide to go for the MA or higher.

Yesterday I ran into Lor. She was standing by one of the kiosks in the plaza, studying the postings. How she could make heads or tails out of those notes jammed together I didn't know. She was dressed in a blue tank top and a pair of old Levis cut off so short that you could see the edge of her panties. She was wearing hiking boots with dark blue socks pulled up to just below her knees. She didn't see me at first. I couldn't help staring at her. Her outfit displayed a hard edge and yet I got a fleeting glimpse of her soft side at dinner. She was nothing like Kim. The contrast of her white-white skin and her blue outfit was large, especially when you added her white blonde cornrows. I had to admit that she had a certain appeal I found at once real and foreign. Don't ask me what that means; well, I'll try. Her legs were as beautifully shaped as her arms and shoulders and neck. Her cheekbones seemed to rise because she was smiling at the messages for some reason. I couldn't help thinking that in a way, strange to me, she looked sexy, almost sensual, and for a moment I began to feel aroused. Luckily, she noticed me which thankfully ended that feeling. She dropped the pile of textbooks and notebooks, ran over to me, threw her arms around my neck and gave me this super wet kiss before she dropped her arms just as suddenly. She stepped back about six inches from my face and gave me this hesitant smile like she had done something wrong. She stood there for what seemed like a minute, then said, "Let's go to the city for dinner tonight. I'll show you what it's really like: 345-7722. Seven o'clock." Then as quickly as she had come, she turned abruptly, gathered her stuff and walked towards Telegraph. I had to scramble to write down her number. As she was crossing the street, Lor threw me a big wave and vanished in the crowd.

I got there at seven-thirty because I had to work until seven and had gone in two hours early. She was sitting on the front porch in the swing when I pulled up, and she jumped down the steps and trotted out to the curb. She carried a Levi jacket and wore all black, a turtleneck and corduroy pants with Italian looking high-heeled boots and a black beret. You can imagine how dramatic this looked against her white skin. She still didn't wear any makeup, but her eyelashes were amazingly long. At first, I thought they were fake.

"Sorry, I had to work until seven."

She climbed in. "I remembered. I knew you weren't a late person." She leaned over and kissed my cheek. I wasn't used to all this kissing.

"You look terrific."

"I like dramatic," she smiled and chuckled.

"Well, you look that too." I was beginning to feel firm again and hoped it wasn't just some misplaced lust.

We chattered on about the first week of school and our classes. I was surprised to learn that she had been studying the kiosk looking for math tutorial jobs since— another surprise—she was a math major and would have ten credits towards her master's when she graduated in late May. She told me about these terrific restaurants on one block at the edge of the ghetto, and I surprised her by already knowing about them.

"Where'd you and this guy Dino meet?" The sixty-four-thousand-dollar question.

"Remember, he was my cellmate."

"I must have been asleep after dinner. The fire I guess." She moved over and put her hand into my crotch. "Who were you expecting?" She really giggled this time and retreated to her side of the seat. Her motion was so

138

natural that I wasn't the least embarrassed. Like it happened every day.

Now I laughed. "Was that your short arms inspection?"

"What's that?"

"Just a military term. Never mind. You're full of surprises."

There was one booth left open in the Japanese restaurant, so we were very lucky. It was like she knew the menu by heart because she never hesitated in ordering, including a Sake for each of us.

"I think the surprises are my kind of insecurity. Just testing to see whether someone likes me."

"You'll have to admit that's a strange way to work out insecurity, but I like it."

"I'm sort of happy and unhappy about sex." She stopped my question. "I'll explain later, if there is a later."

"Ok. Now you asked me about Dino, how I knew these restaurants."

"You don't…."

"No, I want to. You're being pretty honest with me." The Sake came, and we sipped a little in silence. "Dino is a black guy I met in prison, the first black person I ever met. We got to be good friends. Here's the tricky part for you and me. We were cellmates." Her lashes and eyebrows seemed to raise at the same time and her lips parted slightly. "See, I told you."

"No, go ahead." Our food arrived steaming hot.

"I hit my sergeant at the end of boot camp and got court-martialed and sent to prison for a few months. Then, this is the worst, they gave me a dishonorable discharge." I opened my arms wide as if finishing my confession. Lor took my hand and kissed it. I almost spilled the rice on the table.

"That's a great story. I like it. I didn't know you were a tough guy." I was about to protest. "Alright, I know you aren't. I don't even think you know how to be macho. That's what I felt right off, when we first met. I dated a macho type. He was an asshole, but it took a long time to see that. I'll tell you that story sometime." We concentrated on our food and Sake and when we were finished, there was a bunch of people prowling the room looking for who would finish first.

She wanted to listen to some Flamenco guitar and singing. She knew a place just before you went through the Broadway tunnel and up a side street in a bigger storefront with a stage. It was actually a restaurant as well and owned by a family. The son played guitar and his two sisters sang. The guitarist came to our table and kissed Lor's hand and to my surprise, she spoke Spanish with him. He gave me a nod and returned to the stage.

140

"You're even more full of surprises. Spanish?"

She took my hand under the table and weaved our fingers in and out as she talked. "No big deal. My Dad made the whole family speak it. Ever since I was a kid, he would tell us this was a Mexican state and we'd eventually be handicapped without it. We always come here."

"He sounds like an amazing person. I think he's right."

"Who knows? But I'm glad I know it." She let go of my hand. "That's part of a long story. Like your jail time. Maybe I'll tell you."

We were silent then as her friend Paco started on his first number. His speed with the guitar was amazing. He seldom missed a note. After a couple of pieces, his sisters entered and combined flamenco dances with song. The first show lasted about an hour and nobody bugged us for drinks so we both nursed bourbons. Then we left, Lor waving good-bye to all of them including the bartender.

"They all know you."

"Like I said, we come often."

On the way back to the car, we ran into a guy who had the look of a heavy user. His skin seemed to be stretched tight over his nose and cheeks, and there were dark circles under his eyes which were crowded with red veins that spilled out onto his flat nose. Lor walked over to him and touched the labels of his coat. I stayed back as they spoke

141

briefly without introducing him and he continued up towards Columbus. She didn't speak until we turned the corner and headed for the Volvo. "Just a guy I know."

"Looks pretty ragged to me."

"He is. I met him last year in rehab. It looks like it didn't take with him." After that she was silent all the way home across the Oakland Bay Bridge except to say she wanted to see my place.

I was still thinking about the guy we'd seen and how out of context he seemed in comparison to her but, at the same time I felt a little uneasy about her and being in rehab. She settled on the couch, leaned on the far arm and put up her feet. I had just poured our wine and was settling down when she began, full steam ahead. "I used to hang out a bunch in the city, especially in the North Beach-Chinatown neighborhoods. That's where I met all the druggies like Clyde, the guy tonight. It was in my sophomore year when it got really hairy. There's not much to tell. Strung out. Heroin. Knew I was hooked and needed help."

"Amazing you realized it."

"Yeah. Called my parents. We still live out in the avenues near the beach. They registered me in this fancy place in Carmel Valley. You know? Shrinks, group sessions, message, aroma therapy, tai chi, horses, walks and swimming. The whole bit. And lots more than they could afford."

"That must have cost a bundle."

"I went to the same place when I was a junior in high school."

"Your parents sound pretty understanding."

"I think there was a point they just gave up since they wanted a sweet young girl who never got in trouble and went to a private school. Never me! So, they—maybe grudgingly—decided to accept me as what I am. Even I never thought I'd be what I am. I know I've pushed the limit with them, but they're always there for me, God bless'em." She drank some wine and was quiet for a moment. Then she rubbed my leg on the other side of the couch. She looked at me for a long time until I was getting uncomfortable. "Are you okay with what I am?" she almost whispered the question.

I stopped her foot and squeezed it. "Yeah, I'm fine with you though what you are can sometimes surprise me. That's okay too. That's new for me."

That bought on another one of those surprises. She came across the space between us, held my head and looked at me then planted another one of those super wet kisses on me. This time I had to restrain myself from falling on top of her. It took a huge effort not to. Then as before, she backed away as if realizing she's lost control momentarily. "Thank you," she almost squeaked.

We both got up at once as if on cue. Lor put on her jacket and smiled, rolling her head as if savoring the moment. I drove her home. We walked to her porch. She wouldn't let go of my hand until we climbed the stairs and were at the front door. "Great evening. Sorry about my low-life acquaintances. Thanks."

I took her hands again. "How about you coming over sometime next week? We can shop for and cook dinner?" She nodded. "I'll call." I touched her shoulder, turned and went down the steps.

We didn't see each other until the next Saturday. It was only the second week of class, but I was already buried in reading so I could only read two essays in Howard Zinn's book. He took an approach to history that I'd never realized before. It made so much sense to me because he wrote from the perspective of ordinary people instead of the usual crap about kings, queens and so-called esteemed persons. That same level of integrity I'd found in the other authors was here too. He was opening another world as they had. He was writing about the people I felt the Constitution was written for.

I couldn't figure why Lor always waited for me on her front porch, even tonight while it was raining pretty hard. She wore another turtleneck sweater, this time in light brown and matching corduroy pleaded slacks with a baggy look. She carried a large canvas bag but wore no hat. She snuggled close to me as we drove back but didn't pull away this time. We stopped at the supermarket down on Shaddock and picked out our dinner. We decided on chicken, half a baked potato each, and salad. We made a special trip to the health food store by my studio where she painstakingly picked out some gluten-free strawberry pie and organic ice cream. I'd left a Jack Daniels in a glass on my kitchen counter with the bottle and she asked for one too.

She immediately took charge of the kitchen and ordered me onto the couch. She did her work so quietly that you wouldn't know she was handling pots and pans. I sipped my drink and in less than half an hour she said we could eat in an hour after the potato baked. Lor finally sat down on the couch next to me and we shared the rest of our week. She drank her first Jack like it was water, and I got us a second.

"Marco, you wouldn't believe this dufus I have for my Eastern Studies class. Being a math major, I'm used to nerds and cluster heads, but I expect to find a human being breathing in a non-math class."

"Good luck."

She half-cocked her head and looked doubtfully at me. "You get those types too?"

"Yeah, it'd say about ninety percent of the time. No joke. I get very little respect. Much like high school. I'm used to it."

"Lucky I'm terrific at math or I'd be in trouble. Most of 'em couldn't clearly explain the way to the women's head." That I had to laugh at; she was the first girl I'd known who referred to the restroom as the 'head.'

"Why the interest in Eastern Studies?"

"It sounded like an interesting filler. You're not the only one interest in Zen."

"How'd you know that?"

"I looked at the book on your desk last time when you used the head."

"Always full of surprises." I smiled and touched her cheek.

She pressed my hand firmly on her cheek and looked at me with an impish grin. "How about a quickie? An hour 'til dinner." She softly rolled onto me. She made me feel like I wanted to be totally unrestrained, folding myself into her, but I'd never learned how. It wasn't a mad scramble, more of an easy, almost coordinated taking off each other's clothes. But she stopped me when I tried to take off her panties and bra. "Gotta' get the shutters and lights first." So, we raced around closing shutters and could barely make each other out in the little light coming in from the street and rainy twilight. We managed to get the couch rolled out and into bed without hurting ourselves.

We gathered together and then she ok'd the rest of her clothing coming off. "Promise you won't peek." I grunted and lied. I wanted so much to see her and did as my eyes adjusted. I was straddling her hips and looked down at her. She even had that 'cut' in her stomach muscles, and really was a natural blonde which got me even more excited as I kissed her breasts, arms, neck, face and legs. I fumbled with a condom, though she said she was on the pill, and couldn't stop myself from taking the next step and she responded by wrapping her legs high over my ribs. We lay there barely moving for at least ten minutes. It was all I could do to control myself as she whispered, "Marco, Marco!" And then with a fierceness, as if we were at the end, not the beginning it began. We must have broken some record, then it was over.

I couldn't hold myself up and didn't want to crush her, so I rolled off and to the side but she didn't let go of the grip with her legs and we laid there just rubbing each other with me inside her until we settled down and were breathing almost normally again. I worried about the condom holding as we rested.

Then she slowly moved her legs away and went into the bathroom. I turned on the lights and left my robe for her by the bathroom door. I was checking the potatoes and chicken when she came out in the robe. She looked at it and smiled, then wrapped her arms and a leg around me and gave me another wet kiss that added a very wet tongue until she pulled back and looked at me. "Thank you."

"Thank you too." Lor unwrapped herself, got up and added dressing to the salad without stirring it. I pulled her back and felt her breasts under the terrycloth robe. We stood, and I offered to make us another drink. "Maybe we need a little regeneration time," I laughed and so did she. We took our drinks, pulled up the bed and flopped down with a sigh.

"Tell me about Zen."

"I don't know much about it. Mostly from a 'how to' book my friend Dino gave me. It seems to be mainly about meditation."

"We did a lot of that during my rehabs, but I got out of the habit fast when I got out of there. I'm not knocking it. I have friends who swear by it. Have you tried?"

I took another drink. "Yeah, once at my friends Annie and Dave's place. It felt good, quieting."

"You want to try it now. We could after dinner."

The dinner was excellent. Lor had let the steak set in a great sauce for a while and it was a perfect match with the potato and salad. I didn't know what 'gluten-free' meant until she explained it, and it still tasted good. After the meal, we did the dishes and then went back into the couch to do our meditation. We sat cross-legged in the middle of it facing each other. I was tempted to reach out to her but realized from her closed eyes that she was taking it more seriously than me. I was having a lot of trouble concentrating

with her that close but managed to sit still for a half hour
when she got up and went to the bathroom to put on her
clothes.

When she came out she was ready to go. "I'm a less
is more person when it comes to sex. I hope you'll
understand."

"I do…understand. But what about this 'in the dark'
thing? Where'd that come from?"

I helped her with her raincoat though the rain had
stopped. "It's a short story that has a crappy ending. I'll tell
you when the time is right, okay?"

I nodded as we went out the door, wondering how
someone who looked as terrific as her would not want to
show herself, especially when you're in a loving setting?

I drove her home. "I'm gonna' sleep tonight." She
squeezed my arm.

"Me too."

When we got to the porch she did the same thing,
arms around my neck and a kiss. "A guy in the city I know
whose Dad does some work with mine is having a party,
even a little jazz group, next Saturday. It'll be on Russian
Hill at a condo his uncle lent him. Is that okay?"

This time I kissed her back and she returned it
instead of moving away. "Sounds fine to me. May we'll run
into each other this week on campus." She kissed me again,
we hugged, and she opened the door.

149

chapter nineteen

We ran into each other only once on Thursday of the next week and she reminded me of the Saturday night party. Before we met that day, she had put up over fifty "Right to Choose" posters on bulletin boards and kiosks around the campus. She thrust one at me and I was made to promise that it would be in my campus side window. In our conversation, she explained how her family had lived in Mexico City when her father was sent there for two years to teach math and that's where she had learned to speak Spanish. I pointed out the irony between believing in a 'right to choose' and living in an anti-right to choose country. She said I was being dumb and stuck out her tongue at me as she was leaving, but then seemed to change her mind and kissed me on the ear and was gone.

We got to the party about nine-thirty and from the number of cars parked around the large entryway to the high rise condo on Russian Hill it looked like it was pretty much in full swing. We didn't have to look for a parking space because they had a valet who told us that he had the right to get us a cab if we needed it when we came out, and Lor signed a paper to that affect.

"Pretty fancy," I remarked as we walked to the door.

"His father's friend has tons of money. They seldom use this. Wait 'til you see the condo."

150

By now, I could afford a very nice Harris Tweed sport coat, dark slacks, white shirt and knit tie. Lor wore a modestly cut long black expensive looking dress that she swore she made, and high heels. She looked stunning with the contrast of that color against her hair and skin. As we waited on the elevator, I saw the number of stares she got. Before going up, a bouncer type individual, also in a tux, asked for our IDs and politely checked our names off his clipboard list. In the elevator I whispered, "With security like this, what are they expecting?"

"Probably the cops. You'll see. Broaden your education"

I put my arm gently around her. "You're already doing that." She didn't have time to reply because the elevator opened on the fifteenth floor and we all got out. To me, it felt like stepping onto another planet. Our IDs were checked again. The party was in what I guessed was the living room through white framed open glass doors. Large would be an understatement. The room ran the length of the building. There were two bars—and this is where the other planet comes in—the first was to the right as you entered the living room and must have been the dining room without the party. People were on every stool. Waiters and waitresses were picking up drinks and trays of champagne at the one end and practically running back into the twenty-foot high living room, disappearing into the crowd. It was the other bar that knocked me out. I guess I'd led a sheltered life because the so-called bartender there was running lines of coke on small trays and filling meth pipes.

Lor saw my astonishment and hugged my arm. "My innocent guy." Which said it all. We mingled for a while. She introduced me to the host and I didn't feel underdressed when we met because he was wearing a black tee shirt. It was painfully obvious that he had a 'thing' for Lor but seemed to realize it wasn't going anywhere.

To blend in, I decided we needed a drink and went to the bar for two Jacks on ice. I was embarrassed to order ginger ale! I had a heck of a time in the traffic jam finding her, but she was by the windows that looked out on the Golden Gate Bridge and waved me over. She was standing by a high cocktail table with hors d'oeuvres, empty glasses and an empty tray that had once held lines of coke which I hoped she hadn't taken. I handed her the drink. "We straight?" She took a big swallow and shook her head 'yes' and 'no.'

We danced and mingled some more and kept losing each other and then getting together again. Each time she seemed a little more out of it and, given her history, she worried me until I finally cornered her and forced her to pay attention to me. "No joke. I think we need to leave." She pursed her lips and her lower lip dropped just slightly as if she knew she needed to pay attention to me.

"Yeah, you're right. I…I'm sorry, really." Without hesitation, she took my arm and we wedged through the crowd to the front entry where another bouncer type in a tux gave us her coat. We managed to pass the scrutiny of the one with the clipboard, and our car was bought up from somewhere. It was easy getting back on the bridge to Berkeley even with the Saturday night traffic. We got to my place just past twelve. She wanted to have a nightcap before going home.

She dropped onto the couch and I got us two white wines. We sat apart, leaning on the arms of the couch. "Before you say anything. I'm really, really sorry. It was just the setting. All those trust fund babies with nothing to do but party. I got caught up. All that uncontrolled money makes me both sick and insecure…." She looked at me with this pensive, hesitant look. "I really am really, really sorry. Will you….?"

I held up my hand. "Please, don't say it. You know that answer, but I also admit that it kind of scares me. How much did you have?"

Lor stared out the window as if she didn't want to answer. "OK. I had small meth pipe and one line of coke. Not a lot."

I moved next to her. "You may not think it's a lot."

She shook her head in frustration. "I know. I know."

Then I started caressing her hand and forearm. "Can you tell me why?"

"I think I know….and then I don't." She put her other hand over mine.

"I think it was the first time I was strung out and before I went to rehab." She paused. I could plainly see it was awful for her to recall, let alone talk about. "I was only fourteen and was running around with this senior who got me into it because I wanted to be with the "'in crowd.'" She made a 'quotation' sign with her fingers. This one night I got really high, more than ever, and this guy…" She began to cry slowly.

"You don't have to go on, Lor, you don't." Now I was kissing the palm of her hand.

"No…no…I want to tell you. I want you to know. I'm just afraid you won't care after I do."

"Bullshit."

She was quiet for maybe five minutes. The tears kept coming. "I can say it well enough, but I can't tell you how horrifying it was. This guy was way high and so were his friends, and three of them raped me. I tried to fight. I wasn't so high that I didn't know what was happening, but I couldn't fight them off. I called my Mom after and she came and took me home. Right after that I was in rehab." I let her cry and just kept messaging and squeezing her hand until she stopped, and she wiped her eyes and face. She looked at me

tentatively, as if I was going to chastise her. "Could you
handle that?" Lor said, even more tentatively.

I reached up and stroked her cheek and smiled. We
sat like that for a few minutes and then she gently nuzzled
over and rested her head on my shoulder. It was almost one
thirty when I glanced at the clock. "God, I wish I could make
you understand how much more you are than that bunch
tonight. I know you know that in some way already, but
maybe you haven't gotten it emotionally yet. Those people
can't hold a candle to you. You're so much more alive than
they will ever hope to be, no matter how much shit they take
in, no matter how many times they get high. I wish more
than anything that I could show you that." I was feeling
those emotions so strongly, it surprised me. "I've never felt
this way with anyone before. As far as I'm concerned,
you've got it all and more. I mean it." I kissed her corn
rows, her forehead, her nose. I couldn't stop.

She held her head up and looked at me. "Are...are
you sure?"

"What do I have to do to make you believe me? The
only thing I can't do is make you believe too. And I do have
some idea how hard that is. Come on, let's go to sleep."

"Shouldn't I go home?"

"You get to make breakfast in the morning." I
grinned. "What I can't understand is why we made love. I
would think that's the last thing you want to do, ever."

She managed a small smile. "For some reason I don't understand, it didn't affect me that way, not completely. It just felt so natural with you. No, natural isn't the right word. I think it was trust…I felt I could trust someone again, or maybe for the first time. I don't know much about trust. That's why I was so flighty with you…you know the kiss and run stuff. It's like I was touching my toe into unknown waters. I have a hard time explaining. And, I know, there's still the 'lights out' issue which I will tell you about someday. Shouldn't I go home?"

"No. Call them and let them know. We'll have an old-fashioned sleepover." I gave her a silly grin. She kissed my cheek. "Thank you for the trust. That means a lot to me, Lor."

It was a quiet Sunday. I woke around ten and she was already in the kitchen. I could smell the bacon. "Can I help?"

"Yeah. Make the bed and roll up the couch. It's a more comfortable place to eat instead of these kitchen counter stools." I did what she asked and Lor carried in a tray with coffee, fresh orange juice, scrambled eggs, bacon, toast and jam. Even my Mother didn't make scrambled eggs as good as hers.

When we finished, we did the usual kitchen chores together. "Ok, I have a plan," she said opening the couch again. "Here's the deal if you want to. We get into bed in our

tops and bottoms and I tell you what I promised last night....
the lights off thing."

We got into bed as she asked and lay under the quilt.
I always felt sexy in the morning and was having a hard time
not touching her under the quilt. Lor rolled onto her side and
faced me, staring without speaking for what felt like
minutes, but I said nothing.

"I feel more stupid and foolish trying to tell this."

"You don't have to. It's not foolish or stupid I don't
think. In fact, I think it's amazing that you want to even
share it with me."

"Thanks." She paused again and kept staring at me
as if she suddenly couldn't believe me. "I never told my
folks about this because the guy worked with my father. He
had come to a reception at our house in the summer just
before I was a sophomore, fifteen and a half. I don't know
why they always included me at these things. Maybe it was
some kind of 'new parenting,' but I was so out of it with
these groups. Anyway, this guy from his office—a
supervisor—was there. A trash boss, if you will? He was at
least thirty. We ended up sitting in one of the garden swings
and we started talking and hit it off I guess, though I don't
know what we had to talk about. Anyway, you can imagine
'a fellow worker's daughter' had to be taboo, but somehow,
he got my number and called. I think we only went out a
couple of times and he tried to score. I had...never. I turned

him down, but he kept calling. I could have just told my Dad and this guy would have been gone. But I didn't, I guess because I was sort of awed by the idea that some older guy would be interested.

"Well, it happened on the third date because I was kind of drunk. It made me feel less scared if he propositioned me. He at least acted sensitive. But then we started seeing more of each other and that's when things got weird. He kept saying I should get a boob job. Can you imagine what my folks would have said if I came home with that request?" She laughed. "Then, he started making me get up and brush my teeth in the morning before he'd kiss me; stuff like that. And I never even smoked! This went on for about three months. I kind of kept absorbing it unconsciously and slowly identifying with it until I told a close friend about it, Georgia, who I've known since high school. She really tore into me, kind of shocked me awake. It was rough, but she gave me the courage to break it off around Thanksgiving a year ago. I still have this left-over body hang up even though I know I look pretty good. That was when I got back on drugs and into rehab. I guess I'd fallen for him and he really shattered me." Her hand fell across my chest and she looked at me. "I hope that didn't turn you off? I needed to tell you."

It did and didn't turn me off. Did because my ego wanted to say I was first and didn't because even I knew it was a big incident to tell someone, anyone else. I leaned over and gave her a long kiss. She looked a little apprehensive, but I got her to smile by turning the corners of her mouth up with my fingers. She put her arms around my shoulders. "I'm still not over it. I'll really try, promise."

"Alright, but for now its lights out. Unfortunately, its daylight and the shutters don't make it dark. What if I keep my eyes shut?"

"You better." Then she gave me a kiss and I shut my eyes.

The next day was Sunday and we slept off and on, but both awoke feeling relaxed. We lay there listening to the random cars that passed below my windows. She finally rolled over and pressed her breasts against my arm. "Be honest. Do you think they're okay?"

I gently touched them with my other hand. "Honestly? Absolutely. Big breasts are another American macho myth, I think. It's hard for me to understand this whole thing. Most women would die for a body like yours. I wish I could make you see that."

"I was awfully young when it happened. It somehow sunk in. I'm sorry."

Lor still looked at me with a little apprehension. "You up for a way over this?" She nodded. "Okay, here's my idea, and you don't have to do it unless you want. We'll do the lights out until you take me seriously when I tell you

how great you look. I'll put a hundred on it that you will."
She laid back on the pillow and stretched her arms over her
head to show her breasts, then as quickly pulled up the quilt.

"Wow, that was a great beginning!" We both
laughed.

Suddenly, the subject changed. She asked if I would
go with her to support Planned Parenthood the next Sunday
afternoon and then go to the city and meet her folks and have
dinner with them. Both proposals made me slightly uneasy:
the former because I believed in a woman's right to choose
but didn't know if I could stand up for it in public: the later
because parents like hers who I knew loved Lor scared me,
and I worried about being tongue-tied. I said yes, come what
may.

chapter twenty

It was cold and sunny when we drove to the Planned Parenthood location in a fringe part of Oakland the next Sunday. We were carrying support signs but were really there to protect anyone entering the facility which was a large building with a parking lot in front. Sunday was the main day the abortions took place because it was least frequented by protestors who ranged from radical right groups to fundamentalist Christians. I parked well down the street because I envisioned some nut keying my car or breaking a window, which I realized was stupid, as we walked the two blocks to the center, because how would they know my car?

I was surprised to see a dozen "Don't Kill a Human Being" and other signs on the sidewalk and in the street. We tried to be casual as we walked to the front entrance for our briefing, but Lor with her white-blonde corn rows didn't exactly blend in. They told us not to speak with the protestors or engage them in any way. If there was any trouble, the center had a special line with the police.

By the time we got to the edge of the parking lot by the sidewalk, there were at least thirty protestors. In about ten minutes the first patient drove or was driven into the lot amidst screams of "baby killer!" and "you can still repent, and Jesus will love you." Luckily, there were no real problems as the clients parked and were led immediately inside. As you can imagine by now, Lor never ceased to amaze me. And this was another one of those times. We were walking close together, and I noticed that she was smiling at each of the protestors as we passed them. The truly amazing part was that many of them smiled back.

When everyone had arrived, we came back into the center, were thanked and turned in our signs. On the way out, we expected to see the protestors still there, but the street and sidewalk were empty as if they'd been on a movie set and the director had yelled "that's a wrap." I was also pleased to find my dear, old Volvo undamaged.

When I'd picked her up, Lor had teased me because I had worn a tie and my new white shirt with my sports coat. Defensively I remarked, "My Mother is really pretty informal. Actually, not a bad quality." But that thought continued on my mind as we drove across the bridge and, with her excellent directions, easily found our way out to the avenues where she lived and had been born. All the way there, she kept reassuring me that everything would be fine, don't worry. I wasn't as nervous as I thought I'd be.

Their house, being out in the avenues, was identical to lots of houses in that section of town. They were built wall against wall, had a single car garage and small lawn and garden space, a downstairs room that led to the small rear yard and the rest of the house was on a second level with the kitchen and living areas in the middle and bedrooms in back. Some like theirs were three bedrooms because she had an older sister who worked for a non-profit in Washington D.C., a younger brother who was on scholarship at some Ivy League school, an older brother who was a career Marine captain and Lor. I told her when we'd talked about it that other than her, she had a pretty All-American family. She had gotten sore and demanded that she be included in the 'All-American.' I told her 'no way' but she wouldn't take 'no' for an answer.

Her brothers and sister weren't there so it was her mother and father who greeted us at the front door. Lor was more than right; they greeted us with big smiles like we'd returned from some distant and exotic adventure. It really did feel like a family.

Immediately, her Dad invited me downstairs to a small brick patio off a garage door that opened both ways, street front and back yard, for easy access. He offered me a beer from a cooler and started wrapping chicken in foil. The BBQ was space aged because it had an interior oven and an exterior grill, both powered by Propane.

"Wait 'til you taste this chicken. When you do it in foil all the juices stay inside, and I guarantee you'll want more than one piece."

"That's a pretty fancy set up."

"Yeah, all the bells and whistles. We've only had it a couple years. The guys at the meat packing plant got it for me as a 'goodbye' gift. I couldn't believe I'd been there twenty years."

"Lor…"

"Mark," he interrupted, "Do me a favor, a father's favor?"

"Sure."

"Call her Taylor around us. Her mother tolerates it, but I can't stand someone wanting to be called 'Lor' when she has a beautiful, stunning I'd say, first name. She decided on that just after she got out of rehab the first time and she hasn't let go of it. That's something she actually stuck to."

"Happy to oblige. She told me you worked for the city driving a truck."

Mr. Alway, he insisted I call them Mallie and Jack, finished the wrapping of the corn and chicken and put them gently on a tray in the oven, as if the gentle touch had to be part of the cooking. "That's right. Lor finally outgrew the shame," he laughed, "when she got to Berkeley. She thought it was beneath me to be picking up city waste bins around downtown. She got real democratic since she's been there. Before that in high school, damn, you couldn't live with her."

"I would never have guessed that. She's so unique, so out there. I'd have thought just the opposite."

"Don't get me wrong, she was never ashamed of me, just the job. She's one of the most loving people I've known. Always stood up for me if a high schooler made some remark." I nodded. "But those are the two jobs I worked as the kids were growing up. The night meat job laid the foundation for all their education. We never spent a dime of that money. It all went into college savings. And we did it. As to the trash job, lots of people would be happy to have it, given the pay and benefits for seeing the sights every day with my partner of twenty-two years. It's been a no brainer and in three more years I'll get a pension that will keep me and Mallie very secure. We may even move. We've also got this house and a duplex that's had the same tenants for fifteen years and brings us an additional paycheck each month."

He went on, "I maybe could have done better. Was a reserve captain with a college degree when I finished my four years in the Marines, but we've accomplished all we needed to without some fancy job. I taught math for a few years in Mexico but didn't like the politics. We're proud of the kids. I think they're all gonna' make it." He had finished his duties now and motioned me into chairs in the shade of the yard's one tree, an elm. We were still nursing our first beer. He offered me some peanuts in a dish.

"It sure sounds like it." After a long pause, filled self-consciously by a mouthful of peanuts followed by swigs of beer, I sensed he wanted to say something but wasn't sure how to offer it. Finally, he shifted in his chair so it was closer to facing me.

"Can we talk?" He looked a little uncomfortable.

"Yeah, Jack. Anything."

"I hope you will take this as the view of a concerned father and hear me out." I motioned for him to continue. "She's the baby girl and—don't tell a living soul, please—she has always been my favorite. Mallie and I have encouraged all our kids to think for themselves as best they can. And far and away, she's the one who thinks for herself. Don't ask me why or how, that's just the way it turned out.

The problems began in her ninth-grade year. We were always getting notes from teachers saying that she was too outspoken, but we never discouraged her. And as you well know," he smiled. "that hasn't changed. But it has some. You wouldn't know that because you didn't know her before…before the…" he suddenly pulled out his handkerchief and wiped both eyes. "I…I can't even say it, even after all these years. All I can say is that she instantly shut down. When she was able to go back to school, expressing herself, all her confidence seemed to have disappeared."

"A woman goes through something as horrifying as that, Jack, it's more than understandable. What's amazing is how she came through it at all."

"That's the reason I wanted to talk. You've been going together for a few months, right?" I nodded. "I don't know if she's really ever come back. And that doesn't even include whatever shit she went through with that scumbag at my work. When I eventually found out, Mallie stopped me from punching him out because he was in management and it wouldn't have changed anything. I'm sure you're wondering why we're talking since you two have only known each other a few months?"

"Yeah, you're right." I drank some beer since I didn't know what to say.

"She'd really be mad if she knew we were talking about this because she has an amazingly different attitude toward you. In fact, you're honestly the first person she has gone out with for more than a few weeks." Jack leaned over and touched my shoulder. "She feels close to you. I think she actually trusts you."

"Jack, I first thought she was a little nutty when out of nowhere she comes up to me, almost a stranger except for the class we took last year and asks me to her house for dinner. We've seen each other for just over three months and I'll tell you, Jack, at least from my side I feel closer to her all the time."

"She's beautiful and smart."
"To put it mildly." Then we both laughed. It was more like two guys talking about a girl, not a guy and the girl's father!

"She also has the most unique personality I've ever known. She keeps me on my toes and then some, and a lot of that is because she's so full of surprises."

"The surprises are really what I sat you down for, Mark. I didn't know how to talk to you. Figured I was just a nosey, meddling Dad and you'd take it all wrong. But I see you haven't, and though I just met you, I can see why she actually told her mother and me that she likes you."

"I appreciate you saying that, Jack."

"It's the drug thing, the two rehabs I wanted to talk to you about. Fair enough?"

I raised my hand to indicate that he go on ahead.

"She appears to be in touch and in control, but she's actually not so in touch and somewhat timid."

"I know." Jack adjusted the BBQ.

"Then you're more perceptive than I could have imagined after only knowing her for three months or so. You see my concern. She's still innocent after being…I'm sorry I can't say it. And after this asshole at work who just used her without any real thought for her, a very sensitive kid."

"But in her defense, Jack, you can see the age infatuation with this clown at your work?"

"Yeah, but I don't have a shred of forgiveness for him."

"I wouldn't expect you would, given what happened. It was just your standard male macho bullshit. And just so you know, I've put a bullet between his eyes in my daydreams many times."

He smiled. "Goddamn it, so have I! I catch that sonofabitch in a dark alley and I'll break his arms, knees and all his ribs!" He took a long drink, then laughed. "I'm not kidding."

"I know you're not."

He stared at me. "Tell me honestly, how do you feel about Taylor? No bullshit, be honest. I hope I'm being fair, not prying. I'm her Dad."

Where it came from I didn't know, but it wasn't the one beer. I blurted, "I goddam love her! That's what I believe, Jack. She's not just unique, she's precious." I almost cried when I said it.

"Jesus, you do love her!"

"Yeah, but I'm this fuck up who dropped out of school and got a dishonorable discharge from the Marines. What can I give her, a post office career? And I really don't know what I can or want to do. Yeah, I've got some good qualities, but I have trouble believing in them. I have trouble accepting praise, so I'm a little like Taylor in that sense. I won't bore you, but it all started when I was a kid and I haven't gotten past that yet. See why I'm not such a good pick for Taylor?" I looked away from his eyes in frustration.

Jack reached out and pressed my shoulder hard. "Christ, but you are honest, Mark. In my book that makes up for any shortcomings you may think you have. I know you'll settle on something. After all, if I can make a good living as a garbage man, you can do better than that."

"Okay, but what?"

"It'll come, don't push it. Believe me you've got the makings of a guy who will do something good. You've still got some school yet, a semester or more, right? Let it pass now."

I nodded and shook his hand. "I got it. Now let's go back to your concerns about Taylor."

"This is also between us?" I motioned in the affirmative. "I've felt this change in her over the last few months which I attribute to meeting you, even if that scares you. She's more like she was. She's smartassing and not so withdrawn as she was after each rehab. Mallie agrees with me. But we worry that she's still fragile and can't take any more disappointments. As much as it worries us, we think another one would do her in. I'm sure you get what I mean? The frustrating part is we can't figure where this, 'despair' as she calls it, came from. She's been used to nothing but love and support."

"I swear to you I would never do anything to hurt her. Like I said, she's too unique and precious and beautiful! I may not be able to know my demons yet, but I do know I would never betray her." I grasped his hands. "Please believe me."

Jack nodded vigorously and smiled for the first time. "I believe you wouldn't hurt her."

We were interrupted as Taylor and Mallie came down the stairs to the patio. Lor had put on her short-short Levis. Again, the panties were visible and fire engine red. They both carried a glass of rose wine. Jack and I pulled up two more patio chairs and we sat in a kind of half circle away from the BBQ.

"What have you been up to? It looks like to no good," Mallie teased us.

"Well, I'd say we got to know each other pretty darn fast. And so far, and I hope you concur Mark?" I gave a thumbs-up. "So far we're doing fine!"

"Has he told you how bad I am?" Taylor asked half-jokingly.

"Yeah, and it just about knocked me out." I laughed. She got up and kissed her Dad warmly on the cheek. The way he looked at her, I could tell how he felt.

"She's Daddy's girl, all right." Mallie laughed.

Jack stood and raised his beer. "A toast to Taylor."

Mallie did the same. "And one to Mark, who is instantly likeable."

"Thank you and I hope you'll keep liking me." We all laughed. I looked at Lor. "And I hope she keeps liking me." I toasted her again and so did they. Lor smiled, hesitated and stuck her tongue out at me. "Ah, is that a form of endearment?" We all broke up again.

Jack got up and went to the grill. "I'd say those shorts are a kind of endearment." He rustled Lor's corn rows. "My lord, I never thought civil rights would get this close to home." He opened the grill and Mallie signaled us to help set the plastic utensils on the wooden picnic table. We put our drinks down. Lor and I were sitting on one side and her parents on the other. Jack served us on paper plates and napkins. We toasted again and dug into the great smelling food.

"Taylor tells us you're interested in English, Mark. Are you thinking of doing some kind of writing?"

"No, I just like reading. I only got into it when I came back to Cal and a friend of mine turned me onto some authors I'd never heard of. Right now, I'd say I wouldn't make a career out of English. I still haven't figured that out."

"Well, Taylor says you're taking another semester or so to finish. Maybe something will turn up that's least expected?"

"I can get you a job driving a garbage truck," Jack interjected with a laugh.

"The kind of money he makes, don't laugh." Mallie affirmed.

"I think it would be fun driving around downtown, clear sky, fresh air, no deadly office work. I can see it."

Mallie frowned. "I don't want to encourage you,
Mark."

"The Cal grad. with his toy garbage truck!" Lor
kidded. I leaned over and kissed her cheek.

"I've been reading a lot about a guy who is a poet,
worked for the forest service on the roads and as a lookout in
the summer. Sounded like an exciting way to make a living."

"Yeah, if you're single." Lor added and sort of
growled.

"Oh, I don't know." Mallie glanced affectionately at
Jack. "Having a husband away isn't so bad." And then broke
into near hysterical laughter.

That's how the rest of the dinner went: lots of back
and forth jabs that we all took part in, just as if I was a long-
lost son who'd come home from Vietnam alive.

We talked about the evening together as we drove
home. She had moved close to me and wouldn't let go of my
arm which made it a little difficult to drive, but I had no
objections. Lor had been strangely quiet except to agree with
me that her parents were really rare, supportive and
understanding and that's why she loved them. I said I'd
fallen in love with them too. We were quiet again. I should
have been ready for one of her impromptu surprises. She
spoke almost timidly, like she feared the answer but was still
going to ask.

"Can we live together now?"

I realized that this is what I had hoped for in the back of my "Yeah, but" mind that suddenly went "cut the shit" and I forced a happiness into me and, hopefully over to her.

"That's the best surprise you've given me, ever." We kissed on the lips and I nearly went off the road.

"But wait, please." She almost pleaded.

"What?"

"I want to talk about drugs."

"Ok." And we continued to, up to getting into bed—her in the red underwear and one of my white tee shirts and me in my tee shirt and boxers. We'd propped up the pillows. Our legs were under the quilt. We both had a big glass of red wine. Out the front window, the white fog was almost to the ground.

"I'll ask again for the tenth time, what if I do it again?"

"You know your parents and I will be there for you, no question."

"Then why didn't I stop?"

"Because you didn't want to, Lor, Sweetheart. I don't know why. Only you can know that and maybe it's still hidden from you."

She was crying, and the wine spilled a little on the quilt. "But I don't want to be some fucked up junkie! Don't you believe that?"

"Christ! I believe it wholeheartedly."

"And are you willing to take the risk?"

"Of course. God, don't you know how beautiful you are? Inside and out? Look how kind you are to people. Look how loving you are to me and your folks. You'll never be a fucked-up junkie, never!"

She took a sip and set the wine down on the lamp table then pulled herself over and nestled on my chest. "I'm tired of talking, if that's okay." She turned out the light and lay back against me, pulling herself under the quilt. "Are you sure you want to move in with me?" Her voice was muffled by the quilt.

"Yes, yes, yes, a thousand times yes. I'll call Paul tomorrow and see if he has a two-bedroom coming up for rent."

chapter twenty-one

The high points of our life together began when Paul said he had a two-bedroom vacant and was repairing and fixing it up. It would be available in three weeks. Yes, we could have it. Just four hundred twenty a month! It was a beautiful cottage with grass and flower beds and old trees, and we had our own private backyard that looked off toward the Berkeley hills. Jack and Mallie volunteered a nice queen-sized bed and dresser along with a big Oriental rug for the living room. Paul and his wife, Flora, had an old kitchen table and chairs, and we found a green leather chair in a local resale shop in excellent condition.

There was a long-abandoned table in the garage that we refinished and made into a desk for both of us. Happily, Lor was a "less is more" person in sex and furniture so we had no clutter. For indoor life, we bought some house plants, and in less than a month we had a home. Luckily for me, the "less is more" idea on sex would slowly continue to diminish though the "lights out" deal persisted but showed signs of slowly fading more.

We started an invitation on Thursday nights that turned into a welcome routine—we had her folks over for dinner, potluck, and they brought a bottle of wine. Moving in together, I had three surprises, one expected and two not. First, she was so much more relaxed with me in every way but intimacy, which was still blocked by the "lights off" routine. Second, we became very studious, even reviewing each other's assignments when I got home at nine-thirty and seldom dropping off to sleep before midnight. Third, it was hard as hell to accept, but I guessed I was really beginning to feel what happiness was, without worrying it would be taken from me. Lor affirmed that, so I knew I was right.

Yet it was still difficult. It was as if we were each trying to find affirmation in an environment that itself was already affirming us. She was becoming less restrained because there were nights, though rare, when the dim bed lamp was still on she'd come into the bedroom completely naked, get on the bed, sit up on her knees with her arms at her sides and look at me. That would obviously drive me a little insane, but I always restrained myself because I knew how much effort it had taken her to do that. Then she'd put on her "shorty" nightgown and quickly climb in next to me.

I'd caress her cheek. "I know what that took, believe me." She affirmed with a quick nod. And maybe there was even a fourth surprise; we were talking freely about love, a word I'd only mentioned once when I blurted it out to Jack. It had to be love because she'd spend every Saturday when I got home from my route teaching me various degrees of math. I went into it kicking and screaming but kept at it because she believed it was important for a liberal arts person to expand his liberal arts into math. Honestly, I was a pretty bad student, but she persisted.

The best part of that time were the weekends after my work when we'd decide to take a picnic up a trail into the Berkeley Hills and just lay back after lunch, talking or laughing or mostly just being together. Most of those days, we'd take in a movie on Telegraph and walk to the health food store for our dinner before lazily meandering through the empty campus and back to our north side cottage. We didn't really have to be doing anything. Just sitting listening to music with each other was enough.

We didn't go into the city much because the drug thing seemed to hang over us. I also tried not to say anything when Lor occasionally would smoke some weed, but that didn't mean I wasn't concerned. In fact, she would always apologize afterwards and even have a quiet cry by herself; I knew that she was worrying about the potential next step. Luckily, it didn't happen often, and the weeks spread into summer without a hitch. I had a single literature course to finish the English BA and decided to be lazy and wait until spring semester to take it. With Lor and me being so studious, I had raised my failure to a 3.2 average so I'd be fairly competitive.

I had a two-week paid vacation from the PO for the summer and we decided to be spontaneous. Lor would tutor the first summer session and then we'd have August to kick back and maybe even go somewhere for a few days. She seemed happy with her tutoring and had even gotten me through Algebra II when I pleaded no contest that I wasn't up to Calculus and she forgave me.

While she seemed happy, I realized that somehow she wasn't and I couldn't understand why since I assumed we were doing fine on all levels. It happened on a Friday night, the last day of her summer school tutoring. She had gone over on BART to visit her Mom in the afternoon. They were going to have their monthly "girl's night out" and she was usually home when I got in from the PO around nine-thirty. But she wasn't there so I called and immediately could hear the concern in Mallie's voice when I said Lor wasn't home yet. She talked to Jack and then he came on the line and said to give it until ten and call them back.

But ten came and she didn't come home. Now I was beginning to worry more, given her history. I called them back and I could tell Mallie's concern had increased. When Jack got on, I told him I was driving over and would look around the North Beach area since we both knew that's where some of her trouble had begun.

I didn't know what I was doing, but I found a parking place near Chinatown and walked thru the alley by City Lights Books to Broadway. It was late enough for everything to be cranked up now, and I was struck with how a woman's nude body and huge breasts seemed to draw so

179

much of America's awareness; everywhere you looked there were billboards and neon with come hither glances and ultra-suggestive poises.

I kept sticking my head into bars, clubs and restaurants looking for the guy she'd talked to a long time ago. His fatigued face was one I'd never forget. I felt like I was on this automatic pilot, almost a daze of worry and fear the more I walked. I was a couple blocks down Broadway when this guy came off the building he was leaning against and kind of shuffle-stepped over to me.

"Hey…you're….you's Lor's dude, aren't ya? How's about given me a loan of a few bucks 'til I get paid Monday?"

I took out my wallet and handed him a five. "You seen her around?"

"Yo, thanks. And no, haven't seen her since I seen her with you. Swear to it."

"Thanks, I gotta find her." I started to walk, and he gently grasped my arm, stopping me.

"There's a crap coffee house up by the church. She once hung there." I nodded and walked away. He stood in the middle of the sidewalk staring at my five as if it were talking to him.

When I got to the coffee shop, the lights flooded the church and a statue of Jesus. Inside the place, I could feel the heavy, dazed almost nasty pressure that floated up from the small marble tables where what I would call the bottom of the barrel sat in pairs that appeared as intimate as a series of confessionals. She was nowhere that I could make out. But there was a phone booth outside and I called Jack and Mallie. He answered the phone with a hesitance that expected the worse. "I can't find her, Jack. I don't know what to do. Jesus, I'm worried sick."

"So are we, Mark. I'm sure you know that. I'd go home and wait, as hard as that is. I know she'll turn up. She always does, believe me."

I hung up feeling no better and drove home. The light was on in our living room which gave me some hope. I opened the door slowly. She was half stretched out on our couch, staring at the ceiling. I knelt next to her and took her hands in mine without speaking. We stayed like that for almost an hour. From her stare, it had to be heroin. She turned and looked at me. "I fucked up again." I hushed her with a finger to my lips, but she wouldn't look away.

"How about a shower and some coffee?" I leaned over and kissed her cheek and she puckered her lips as if kissing me back.

"I can't make it alone....to the shower."

"No sweat. I'll help you and make coffee while you're in there." I got her up and into the bathroom. "I'll close my eyes, let me help you." And she did, and I did and managed to get her in and adjusted the water temperature for her.

"I won't fall. I…. I'm okay. Go make the coffee."

I hurried making it, then called Jack and Mallie. They insisted on coming over. I went back in to see how she was doing, and Lor was drying her hair and dressed in a bathrobe. She looked at me again. "That feels better. I…I fucked up big time again." I guided her to the couch, set her down and went to get the coffee and a sweet roll left over from breakfast. She slowly but gratefully drank the coffee and nibbled the sweet roll. "It wasn't much. I swear. Honest."

"What was, was. Your Mom and Dad are coming. I couldn't stop them." She shook her head, understanding. "Enjoy your coffee."

"Why are you being so nice? You should be pissed and balling me out."

"It happened, nothing's going to change that. You're safe, home. Isn't that all that matters?" I started a fire in our beautiful fireplace and I moved next to her, putting my arm around her. It took her a while to press against me, but she finally did. I could barely hear her whisper when she asked, "How do you put up with this shit?" but I said nothing, held her and gazed at the fire.

Mallie and Jack arrived. She got off the couch and hugged them through her tears. Jack said, "Taylor our love, what can we do to make it stop?" She hugged him again and they sat opposite us with the fire between.

She didn't stop crying and spoke through her tears. "It's almost like a magnet, it draws me in and I don't want to resist it. It's hell. I...I'm sorry to all of you. You are too good to go through this shit that doesn't seem to have an answer. Maybe once you're on it you never get off."

I interrupted. "BS, I won't buy that. I refuse to."

"We're all here for you, Taylor. God, let us help if we can," Mallie pleaded.

"I'm okay now. I'm back. I'm just so damn sorry."

What choices did we have?

chapter twenty-two

Though we pledged spontaneity to each other, Lor and I were only semi-spontaneous when I took my two weeks off the end of August just before she'd start her senior year and I'd be finished with my BA in the second semester. Both of us had saved some, because while we liked to hike, we also shared the desire not to camp out.

Dave had an old Harley gathering dust in his garage and he let me use it because Lor had wanted to "do the motorcycle thing." I insisted she read Robert M. Pirsig's *Zen and the Art of...* since I'd already read it three times and was still working on it, but she promised another time and from her scrunched-up nose and squinted eyes, I figured it'd be a cold day in hell when that happened. I had a mechanic I knew from my PO route who checked Dave's Harley over and got it back in road condition plus a wash. We were proud of how light we packed, since everything fit in the two leather pouches on the bike.

We left just after the rush across Golden Gate Bridge, so the road was very clear and uncrowded both ways. Taking Highway One, we stayed as close to the coast as possible and pulled into Mendocino just before noon. Being near the end of summer and a Monday, we found the coastal town like we imagined it was fifty years ago. The forest on the hills inland had not been touched, and except for the arts and crafts aspect of many stores—products of a sixties migration north—it still had the wood and stone flavor of the late 1800's. There remained a couple of cafes and diners where the locals hung out, mixed with the more contemporary upscale tourist look. After a great lunch in a locals' place, we found a fifty-year-old hotel, unloaded and decided to take a leisurely walk through the town's few streets. Lor had been straight for several weeks and I was hoping for the best, trying to assume it.

Even in Mendocino, she got her share of stares with the white-blonde corn rows. It was funny but also beautiful when she'd just been "observed," usually by men and we'd be on the street again. She'd give me this seductive smile, shake her hair and grab my hand and kiss it. For me, I'd never had such ongoing affirmation, even if I didn't know exactly how to take it in.

The next two days, we'd get a bottle of wine and lunch at the local diner, put it in our leather pouches and drive every backroad we could find, some private, until we were ready to find a tree and patch of grass to sit on. We'd spent at least two or three hours eating, drinking, gazing at the rolling land or ocean, when we could see it, and did a pretty good amount of nuzzling in silence. If I could have, I'd have settled down right there with her and thought I could be happy, even later when I had to admit that the wine may have had something to do with it.

The little town had given up all the beauty it had for us and we drove north to spend two days in Crescent City walking through the redwoods. From there, we returned home for a night, and headed south to Big Sur. Lor had seldom spent time there and was anxious to see it. She seemed to be doing fine.

We skipped Carmel but promised to come back later for at least a day and a meal and we kept heading south as the road got more narrow and the forest more impending above us. We were having great motorcycle weather and hoped it would hold.

At the south end of Big Sur, I pulled into the gravel lot of the two-story general store that a guy I'd known as a freshman had recommended. He was still living in the city and working on a cable car, even after four years out of college. He'd phoned ahead and told the store owners about us.

Manford and Ilene were both at the counter, but the store was empty. They seemed to do a double blink when we entered, and they saw Lor, but turned it into a smile. "Hi, welcome," Ilene said. We told them who recommended us, and they recognized Ted instantly.

"This is such a beautiful store. It looks like it's been around forever." Lor smiled and picked up a red licorice stick in a counter jar and started chewing on it. "I promise to

pay for it. I just needed something to nibble." They both
laughed.

"Fine with us!" Manford said. "You'll like some of
the real food too. Organic, as best we can make it."

"Ted said your selection was always the greatest.
And homemade ice cream?" They both nodded and pointed
toward the ice cream machine.

Manford took out his register book, found our
name and pointed up the hill and across the street. "I gave
you Ted's cabin. It's at the top, last one, and the trail is just
up behind it. If you follow that, you'll be able to get down to
the beach and there won't be anybody there. We promise."

We figured we'd be there for three days. Ted hadn't
been there for a while and they'd upgraded the stoves and
the showers. We got enough for three days, though they said
we should buy the meat or fish daily when it came in fresh.

The cabin was about a half mile off the road and up
a pretty good hill next to the forest and trail entrance. The
porch had a swing with new looking pads, and you could sit
there and see the distant blue of the Pacific. There were two
studio beds against opposite walls with an ancient leather
couch and table between that faced an even older brick and
stone fireplace filled and ready to light. The small bathroom
had a cast iron tub with a shower. The rear was a nice
kitchen with a granite counter top and all the necessary items
for cooking. The walls were freshly painted white like my

old studio and the ceiling had four by six wooden cross beams stained the color of soft pine and set a couple feet apart. I could see why Ted had loved the place. The closet was a free-standing armoire with a shelf, mirror and drawers below.

Lor bought according to her plans for our meals, including our lunch-hikes, and I helped her put that and our own gear away. We had some lunch and hiked down to the road and from there to the highway, where we crossed and walked through the trees to the cliffs and ocean where a breeze, like an easy massage, washed over us. Lor had been more than her normal quiet and I asked her if everything was okay. For no reason I could figure, she reached over, softly pinched my ear and gave me the kind of smile she did when she wasn't sure that what she was going to say would go over well with me.

"I've just been thinking about you and me mostly. This feels like a honeymoon for some reason. I know that's silly but that's what I've imagined. Different than our trip north." She ran her hands under my shirt collar and kissed my chin. "I'm feeling 'wifie' and, again, don't ask me why or how." She gave me one of her grunt laughs. "Don't worry, boy, I'll get over it. It'll pass. I'm not proposing!"

I grabbed her suddenly and gave her a long hug. "You think, some day?" I smiled, and she shook her head, so I couldn't tell if she was thinking 'yes' or 'no' as we headed back up to the cabin. By the time we got back, showered and put on our sweats, the edge of twilight was burning out in shades of orange toward the sea. As it grew darker, the temperature also dropped, and I lit the fire. "Wonder why that sweet old Norwegian lady dyed her hair back to red?" I mumbled as if to no one. I turned and looked at Lor who gave me a questioning stare from behind the kitchen counter. "She was the neighbor who cured my fear of fire." I passed my hand over the flames. "I love it because of her."

"You never told me that. I never knew you were afraid of fire."

"I was six or seven. Christmas just after my Dad died. A story not worth telling. My mother freaked out and almost caught the tree on fire…and I could feel it—the fear."

She threw me a peeled carrot. "And that's where the Norwegian lady comes in?" I nodded, and she stopped making dinner for a minute, then continued. "And you say *I'm* full of surprises." I ate the carrot and passed my hands over the flames, feeling the warmth rising and covering us.

She had put our steak to soak in her special sauce before we hiked to the cliffs, and I could smell its aroma as she broiled it. We ate on the table in front of the couch with a bottle of red wine Ilene had recommended along with fresh green beans and baked potatoes. We followed Lor's house rule of not talking while we ate. I guess the crack of the dry wood and lick of the flames was saying something to us, but

I wasn't subtle enough to understand it. "Can you hear the fire?" I asked.

"Yeah. It's playing classic music, maybe Bach, in the silence." I reached out and touched her fingers. "I'm serious, mister."

"I got it." Silence again. "I also didn't know who Bach was until I had dinner at your place."

"Now you are joking."

"Scouts honor. I've been listening to music in the library when I study in the music room. We never had music at home. Only my grandmother hogging the television. I did play trombone for a while in junior high yet there was no serious exposure to music. But when you don't know what it is, you don't miss it."

"You lived in a bubble, sort of."

"Yeah." I belched, poured us each more wine and sunk back on the couch. "When you're in a bubble you don't know you're in one."

Lor stretched back onto the couch next to me. We stared at the fire for a long time and it almost put us to sleep. She broke the silence. "But if you know you're in the bubble it must be very painful and isolating, shouting at people but they can't hear you, reaching out but you can't touch them. And they can't care for you."

Coming from her, it seemed out of character. "How do you...?"

"I mean" she interrupted, "I feel like that when my mood goes down. I don't know where I picked it up, the rape or the older guy, but it gave me this isolation feeling and I haven't gotten over it. That's part of what I want to talk to you about tomorrow when we go to the beach, not now. Okay? And my period is just over."

"Yo comprendo."

"Wow, and he speaks Spanish too." She leaned over and kissed my cheek, got up and jumped in to the bed at the left of the fire, propped up her pillow, smiled at me and continued looking at the fire. Just having her close was enough. I drifted off. It was uncomfortable waking from a slouched sleeping position. The fire was embers now, but as I got up I could still see Lor's peaceful face under the quilt. Not a wrinkle, now a blemish, the last of the lipstick on her slightly opened lips. She was lightly snoring; a trait fortunately we had in common. I was going to kiss her but didn't want to wake her. I couldn't conceive of her and hard drugs even for any reason, even the reason she'd just given me. I sat at the table opposite her and kept my eyes on her until I noticed my watch; it was almost 3 a.m. I hoped her beach surprise was a good one.

chapter twenty-three

The next time I looked at my watch it was 5 a.m. She'd already opened the curtains and the first sun fell like a spiraling stream of thin dust across the room. "You said we wanted to leave here by six. I packed a nice lunch of tuna, chips, hardboiled eggs, apples and our water. You get to make breakfast while I shower." I didn't mention that she'd showered last night because I knew she was super clean, another of her qualities that I strangely loved.

"Eggs, beacon, toast, coffee and OJ okay with you?" She waved and closed the bathroom door. I made the eggs scrambled and mixed in hot sauce and cream cheese the way she liked it, and I had everything ready when she came out with her corn rows in a towel.

She sat at the counter and I served us both. "The little people of Oz would love that shower and tub."

"You have to agree that it's functional." Lor nodded.

"Great job on the eggs and bacon." I nodded with a mouthful.

We were out the door by six. It was growing light, but the sun hadn't cleared the forest east of us, only patches of light through the pines and cedars. We got to the beginning of the beach trail, and our boots crunching the gravel became like whispers in the short grass. Lor took the lead. She was wearing the short-short cut-off Levi's and had ignored my suggestion to wear hiking pants.

We moved across the generously wide trail with its downward slope to our right on what would be the ocean side. Something about the size of a fox appeared about a hundred yards in front of us. It stared momentarily, then retraced its steps up the slope. We'd been out an hour with about another hour to reach the downhill branch, according to Manford's calculations.

She glanced back and then stopped, gently sitting on the upward slope and opening one of the waters on her belt, offering me some. I insisting she go first. I sat on a flat rock next to her on the side of the trail. The ocean was just beginning to open to our west, the first distant sound of the surf, barely discernable, drifting up. She rubbed her legs, looking towards the sea. "That was a fox. I always wanted a fox." That was news to me. "They're graceful and intelligent and quick. And with the sweetest eyes."

"Any reason you bring them up?" I asked.

"Just reminded me how easily animals are supposed to shake off danger. You know, one minute they're running for their life and the next sniffing around and grazing, as if the first part never happened. They live so much in the moment, right?"

"I don't know foxes but, yeah, I guess so. Why?"

She got up, put away the water and started down the trail. "I'm getting you ready for my surprise." I followed, puzzled.

As steady as we went, the light increased although we still couldn't see the sun coming over the western hills. We reach the trail's downhill branch and she leaned into the upward sloping pine needles and grass. Her beautiful legs had half a dozen scraps from branches sticking out that she hadn't seen. I sat on the trail itself. "We doing okay?" Lor asked.

"Yeah, terrific from my end but I'm a little scared of your surprise."

She got up almost immediately, smiled and cut down toward the riverbed that would carry us under the highway bridge to the sand. "You won't be scared, promise."

The creek bed was dry this time of year, but there were still a few trickles towards the ocean. Now the first sun came through the forest above us. You could see its brightness against the water. We came out under the highway bridge where the creek ended and immediately took off our shoes and walked in the sand, cooled by the shadows from the cliffs above it.

She looked back at me and her happy glance made me very happy. "I love to see your face looking so happy."

She came back, put her arms around me and we held each other, kind of twisting back and forth, our bodies

194

pressing against each other. "You made me happy. This strange new place makes me happy. I've been to Big Sur twice with my folks and never found this." She looked down the beach. "There's got to be nobody here."

"That's what Manford guaranteed and he delivered."

"I feel like us running naked, if it wasn't for the light. Sorry"

"Yeah, the sun's a sore loser. Let's camp over there where that rise is at the foot of the cliffs."

After she opened the towels and set up our picnic containers and the water, we took off our coats. I rolled up my pants and we started walking along the water's edge. It couldn't have been past eight-thirty. There was a solitude feeling to that beach, as if we'd drifted up onto a deserted island.

No ships passed and there was no movement where the forest touched the sand, nor as far down the coast as we could see. We must've walked five miles down the beach, staying just at the fringe of the surf. We could see a few houses on the cliffs above, but they seemed miles away and with no access to the sand. I don't think we exchanged more than a few words the whole time. We were tired when we got back, so we set out the picnic and ate gratefully and slowly. Afterwards, we stared at the waves. You could hear them, but it was as if they had their own quiet to add to our surroundings. Lor broke our long silence.

"Remember how the fox shakes off danger and comes right back to the moment?" She didn't wait for an answer. "That's the surprise I want to talk to you about."

"How do you mean?"

"My situation with drugs, naturally."

"Can I help?" The sun was warm overhead, but the breeze was light and cool.

"Naturally." She paused for the longest time. "The fox shakes off the experience of danger completely. It's truly gone, forgotten, comes right back to the moment. They've tested this stuff on lots of animals. It's true." She paused again. "I think my situation is that I can shake a 'drug out' off but it's never gone or forgotten. And the shit comes back again but I don't know why…. that's what worries me so much about us. Say I'm fine for a while and it comes back, like it has. How long could you put up with that? It's not like you're Mallie and Jack." She stood and stretched, then sat down again.

"And it's not like they are me, right?"

"What do you mean?" She looked suspiciously at me.

"You know damn well what I mean." I put my hand on top of hers.

Lor half giggled. "I hope I do."

"I think I knew I loved you from the time you invited me to dinner."

"Oh, that can't be true."

"I swear." She leaned over the kissed me. "But I
didn't admit it to myself until later because I thought I was
in love with Kim and was confused. How many times have I
told you that I love you? Hell, even Jack asked my
intentions when I came to the first BBQ."

"What?"

"Yes."

"He asked you?" Then she smiled. "That's my Dad.
And what did you say?"

"I said straight out that I did." This time I kissed
her.

"See, that's why I told you my surprise. It's like I'm
surrounded by love and can't fully realize it. It's why I
worry about another mistake. You understand, don't you?

"I understand why you don't want another mistake
but like you, I don't understand why you'd make another."

"To be continued, maybe." She got up.

"No maybe." We packed and headed up the creek
bed. There was little sun through the forest as we climbed to
the trail branch and we never saw the fox again. We dropped
our gear on the porch and walked to the store. Their son had
dropped by with fresh caught salmon and we had that with
some white wine Ilene again recommended. We added a
delicious green salad, fresh French bread and a couple of
brownies for desert. Lor insisted on cooking again, but I

insisted she didn't, given the long hike. We told them how much we'd enjoyed it. The light was fading when we got back, and she put up the food as I built and lit another fire. Irene had grilled the fish so all we had to do was warm it up with the French bread and our dinner was made.

It was cool, but we bundled up and sat in the swing with our brownie and the rest of the wine. I could not recall a darkness like the one that surrounded us. There were some cabins downhill, but their lights were dim and with no path lights it was like waking up as a kid and feeling the darkness like a protective shield. If the light inside hadn't been on, we wouldn't have been able to make out each other's face. As soon as we had one hand free, Lor grasped mine and we began to rock slowly. Her tenderness always arose a grateful appreciation in me. We would gently squeeze hands now and then as if to assure the other was still there. When we finally finished, she whispered, "There's something I forgot to tell you at the beach."

"Ok."

"It's something about that fox and other animals. It's a quality I don't think many of us have."

"But the animals do?"

She said nothing for a minute, but she may have nodded. It was hard to tell in that darkness.

"I saw a National Geographic wildlife thing as a kid. I never forgot it, just as plain now as it was then. It was filmed in Africa. There was this herd of zebras that was attacked by some lions, and this one had a gnarly bit taken out of her hindquarter. But she escaped and soon was back to grazing with the rest as if nothing had happened. Like that near-death experience no longer registered."

"How do you see that as different from the fox?"

"It's the same, but we never talked about it. I know you must get it."

"I think so. You're saying few of us live completely in the present moment. We're either off in the future or ruminating about the past."

"Yeah, and it sounds so simple."

"But it's hell to impossible to do?"

"Uh huh, and that's the whole point of what I was telling you about the drugs, the moment, the moment."

"So, you're saying they keep pulling you back. That you can't just drop them. But, like you said, how many of us can even approach being in the moment? How could that keep pulling you back, when so few can even live 'now'— even monks I've read about spend years and years practicing?"

Lor squeezed my hand tighter. She wasn't sobbing but she was crying. "Don't you see? I have to come up with something. Otherwise I'm another weak druggie who is never going to pull her life together."

I moved and put my arm around her and let her cry. It was hard to even think about it. It was like another force controlling you.... something you had no real power over like a biological pain that came and went as it pleased and you couldn't figure out how to stop it, but it hurt like hell when it came. She cried for a long time, and when she stopped it was like a child slowly quieting themselves as tears grew less and were finally gone. "You understand now? Really understand?"

"I think I really understand, yes. And I never realized how scary it could be until now. But what I can't figure out is—now don't be mad—what I wonder is whether you've convinced yourself that there's no control or whether somehow you could get control? I mean, look at all these rock stars who had heavy addictions who got clean? I say this because I think you've got more control than you realize, but there's something blocking it, hence, the episodes. Does that make any sense?" She pulled me closer and cried a little more.

"Yes, yes, but that's the whole point, what's blocking me? Oh, God, it's so frustrating. I mean there's nothing I can think of with Mallie and Jack. Of my childhood in general. Nothing."

"We'll just keep pushing, Lor." She got up and pulled me up. The long day and the long talk had exhausted us. We kissed and were asleep long before the embers.

chapter twenty-four

We spent the next morning dawdling over coffee on the porch. Manford came up to tell us that Ilene had baked banana cream pie and was saving two pieces for us for dinner. We seconded that and went back to dawdling until around eleven when we headed south to Nepenthe's for lunch. Being the end of summer, we managed to find a parking place and lucked out on a table for two by the windows that looked to the horizon and down the coast.

We spoke of what Lor would do at the end of the year. She could enter the MA math program and had a good chance of getting into the one at Stanford, but the money was better at Berkeley. When we were up in Mendocino, we visited the forest service office for the state parks. Just for the fun of it, I filled out an application for the next summer. After reading a couple more books by Gary Snyder, who had been a summer lockout in the northwest, his poems sparked my interest in doing something similar. The parks guy said there had been many husband and wife teams, so that would be no problem if I was selected. I spent half a day working on the form with Lor and we hoped when finished, I sounded like Daniel Boone and had spent my previous life in the woods. They would let me know in early May and it would last until early October.

After lunch we sat with glasses of wine on the broad terrace watching the sea. Then we must have spent an hour in the gift shop, where I bought her a piece of Big Sur jade on a necklace.

She happily put it on and said it was never coming off unless it broke. I told her I didn't think the necklace was quality silver, so she might develop 'black neck ring,' a deadly disease of the Congo. It took her a couple minutes to get the joke, and she walked back to the terrace in a huff. But then she forgave me quickly and we drove back to the cabin.

It was about four when we got there, and we shopped for dinner to go with Ilene's pie. We were politely shying away from a tuna, pasta and vegetable casserole dish but Ilene insisted we'd like it and Manford confirmed so we got that, our usual green salad, another white wine Ilene recommended and, of course, the pie. We were leaving the next day, so I promised Lor an early lunch in Carmel and then the drive home.

We lingered and visited, promising to be back. I also squared away our cabin fee, and as we returned to the cabin it was just passing through twilight. After a shower and dinner—the casserole was terrific—we struck a fire as it was chilly outside and then settled with our wine on the couch in our sweats.

"Thanks for bringing me here."

"Thanks for coming. It's been two unique days to me."

"Wanna talk a little more about the fox?" she asked.

"If you want to. You gotta admit it's not easy to talk about for me because I feel so powerless to help or add anything to the subject. You can see that, can't you?"

"Yes, but it just helps that you're listening. You understand?"

"Sure."

"Okay, so unlike the fox, I can't throw the drugs, especially heroin, out of my consciousness. It goes away then pops back later and I don't know why I can't shake it. Oh, I can resist it for months, but then it's like it tires me out and I give up to it." She tossed her head back and forth in frustration. "Oh, the hell with it. Let's not wreck our last night. I shouldn't have bought it up."

"Yes, you should have, and you know it. Listen. I don't want you backing down from this. I don't care how many times it comes up, how often we repeat it. Maybe there's such a thing as the Law of Expanding Returns; the more we go over it, the more we learn." She put down her wine and gave me a long kiss.

"I want to be romantic now."

"Me too but I need to say something. Just put this away for later thought. It just came to me. You've got your reality and your dream reality. My question is why the need for a dream reality when you've got a reality that is full of love and very few people would want to escape from that? No talk now, just put it away and let it simmer. One of these days, we'll talk about the incredible books I've been reading. They're far out. I know you'll be interested."

"Okay."

She kissed me again and this time it was very wet, ranging from the top of my nose to the tip of my chin. Then she got up and took off her sweats, leaving her in red panties and a tee shirt with French sleeves which emphasized the gentle cut in her shoulders and arms. I had a very difficult time restraining myself when I looked at the same gentle cut in her legs. She motioned me to stay where I was which wasn't easy with an erection stuck in my shorts.

She went around and turned out all the lights and closed the drapes. The only light was from the fire and its bright shadows on the ceiling, couch and floor. "Eyes closed," she said, returning to the couch. She sat down in my lap. She was naked. I wanted to cheat again and did a little, but mostly I was pretty good. I tried to run my hands over her body. "Don't do that. I'm making love to my sweetheart, so relax."

Relax! To me, the loveliest woman I've ever seen, and she wants me to relax! Between not touching and not peeking, I was like the guy clinging to the last boulder on the cliff which is about to plunge me into the falls. But I hung on somehow as she caressed every erotic part of my body with her lips and hands and body. When we finally came together, I felt like I'd just erupted from my toes to the top of my head and we lay mingled for several minutes until we fell away in utter exhaustion. After a while, I felt my wine glass against my chin and took it. "Was that romantic enough?" she asked.

"I woulda passed out if there was any more, you incredible sexy and gentle lover." Her hand brushed my shoulder.

"You promised not to peek."

"I'm not!"

"Okay, let's stare at the last of the flames and keep sampling Ilene's second great pick." When the wine was finished, we decided to shower together with just the bathroom door open and my continued vow not to peek. Her skin was so smooth in the touch of hot water and soap. I gave her a towel and we dried, back to back. She reached for my hand and we glided to our separate beds. We kissed once, then lay watching the fire until we were asleep.

chapter twenty-five

We got up early, walked to the store for coffee, juice and a pastry to round out our breakfast. Then back to our swing where we sat, ate and talked until about ten.

I should say I did most of the talking about the books Dino had given me and the ones I had been acquiring since my return to school. It was hard to zero in on specifics that I'd been learning, but in a nutshell, I began to realize that I was being introduced to a new reality, a real material reality as opposed to the dream reality I felt I'd always lived in as I grew. I shared my depression with Lor when I'd realized this because it made my whole life a falsehood without realizing it ever before. The real material reality was something I suddenly understood that I couldn't run from. I even had a dream where I was tied to a stake and my Mother and Grandmother were shouting and hitting my head like a punching bag. That made me more anxious than I'd ever been. I was more anxious because it was like walking into a new experience that no longer was part of the punishment I'd known, yet not solid enough to take hold of. I was identifying more and more with Jack, Mallie and Lor as my family, but even that was not like having my own real family.

I told her how I often felt in a lonely place and because she was so precious, she sympathized with me as best she could, never having known what it was like.

"I've been reading more Zen and practicing meditation. This guy Gary Snyder really got me interested because he actually lived in a monastery in Japan."

"When do you practice?"

"When you're asleep mostly. Sometimes I just sit on a bench between classes with my sunglasses on and do it. I think it's relaxing me."

"Could we do it together sometime?"

"How about now? We can sit for fifteen minutes on the couch. I'd love for us to do it together." And so, we did. And we made a pact to practice every morning before school or work, no matter how we felt. I was happy she wanted to join in.

At ten, we cleaned up and left the cabin for the ride back up to Carmel. We got there in about forty minutes. It was still early and not too crowded yet. We found the Mexican place at the bottom of the main street that Ted had told me about, and we got a nice table near the indoor fountain where only three or four tables were occupied. We ordered a couple of Margaritas with chips, guacamole and salsa followed by cheese enchiladas with beans and rice smothered in a light spicy cheese sauce. We mostly ate, having pretty much talked ourselves out over the last two days.

School began soon, and Lor was already registered for fall semester while I was taking off for a break, so I could work longer hours at the PO job. When we got home, we decided to call Jack and Mallie and invite ourselves over for dinner to discuss what we'd consciously avoided on our trip: taking Lor to meet my Mother and Grandmother. I was pretty shaky and hoped their thoughts might help. Lor wasn't any too steady about the deal either.

We set up the following Friday to have a sit-down dinner with them. It kept coming into my mind all week, and I avoided talking further to Lor about it. But on the real positive side, we were grateful for our spontaneous summer trips and that kept us going until the following Friday.

We had a wonderful dinner, then adjourned to the living room to talk. I decided to lighten the conversation before it started. "On Monday, we want to go to city hall and get married. Will you two be our witnesses?" Even Lor looked surprised.

Jack took it in calmly. "Well, sure." He looked questioningly at Mallie as if to say, 'what the hell?'

"Just trying to keep it light," I broke in as everyone sighed and smiled. Lor did her customary hit on my shoulder to indicate her half-irritation.

"Well, you scared the hell out of Mallie and me. Not the announcement, but the suddenness of it." He laughed. "Okay, we can settle down now." We all nodded.

"The topic for this evening is a visit to my Mother and Grandmother. They gotta' know her sometime. We came for your help."

"How do we help?" Mallie asked.

"We don't know but we need it. Since I've been away, I realize more and more just how alienated I am from them. I'm a long way from figuring out the scars, but I keep trying and I'm still sucked into the guilt and punishment I learned from them. I feel guilty, but I don't want to be around them. And when I think of that, I immediately have this feeling God's going to punish me."

"You'd be amazed at the stories he has from growing up," Lor broke in.

I gave them a pleading look. "I don't know what to do and I don't want Lor hurt in the process of going through the motions of introduction. I don't want to go, and I really think it's crap, but I have this irrational need to do so."

Jack poured himself another glass of red wine and took a drink. "This isn't going to sound like such good advice but here goes. Why not drive down, make the introductions and see what happens. After all, Lor's close to you, they know that by now, right?" I nodded and so did Mallie. "Will that be so hard?"

"I can handle that," Lor said. She grabbed my hand and looked at me with incredible trust. "Can't we?"

"Yes, I think so. The worst that could happen is we'll be thrown out."

"Your mother doesn't sound like the type who'd do that." Mallie said.

So, it was settled. I called my Mother and said we wanted to visit, and she said Saturday would be fine but if we stayed overnight, because of my Grandmother, we'd have to sleep in separate rooms.

We left after my PO route and got to L.A. about four. I think we were both a little scared, so we avoided the subject. I only told her, "Don't be surprised with the way they act." That was the best I could come up with.

There was surely a reason, which I didn't think of at the time, but we left our suitcase in the Volvo at the curb when we walked up the short driveway past the small well-tended lawn to the front porch. As we did, I squeezed her hand briefly as we rang the front doorbell. I was struck for the first time at how small the house was, though it had never seemed that way to me before.

My Mother answered the door in a flower-patterned summer dress. I could see her size up Lor from head to toe with an instant disapproving look at the short light blue dress she wore. But she covered it nicely as she smiled and shook Lor's hand.

"We hoped you could have come sooner but I know you're both working. Come in." I followed Lor inside and kissed my Mother's extended cheek. My Grandmother was sitting in one of the green chairs by the fireplace and didn't get up. I could see the hidden shock coming from them both as they appraised Lor's cornrows. I was dead sure she had picked up on that too, including my Mother's quick glance by the door.

We were herded out the French doors from the living room to the patio in back where the Chinese Elm my father had planted years ago shaded the area from the last of the sun. There was a soft breeze from the ocean through the mountain passes behind the house a couple of miles beyond the backyard. "Would you two like to wash up and then we'll have a cocktail and some dip before dinner." We practically stumbled back inside, and I showed her where the bathroom was and headed for the second one on the other side of the house next to what once had been my bedroom.

Lor was having a white wine and talking to my Mother when I got back out there. My Grandmother was eyeing Lor's legs and hairdo and looked at me with the slightest shake of her head as if to say, "Well, I never in my life." But I ignored that as best I could. She finally interrupted the two of them.

"Lor, is that your real name."

She turned from my Mother. "No, actually my name is Taylor, but I'm usually called Lor."

"I've never hear that name before. Isn't Taylor a boy's name?"

My Mother interrupted. "Please Mother. They just arrived."

"No, that's okay. Sure, it is a boy's name sometimes and sometimes a girl's. It was my great grandmother's name. My Mother, Mallie, wanted me to keep a family name."

"You say your mother's name is 'Mallie?' That's another strange one to me."

"It's actually Morgan, but my Mom never liked that, so she made up Mallie." My Grandmother nodded as if she'd just been told some strange truth from another planet.

"And the girls wear dresses that short in college nowadays?"

"Even shorter." I loved her for holding her own. She didn't give a damn what they thought.

"Whew, back in my day they would have arrested girls dressed like that."

"Mother" my Mother interjected, "times have changed."

"Yeah," I laughed trying to keep it as light as possible. "And no more girdles today." But only Lor picked up on that. Suddenly, I thought we were playing some kind of game like 'The Art of Criticism' and Lor, from her retorts, seemed to agree.

We talked in generalities about her parents and our school and work. They were really taken back when Lor said she was a math major and told them she had started learning advanced math in the fifth grade because her father had been a math teacher when she was small.

"Oh, and what does he do now? Is he retired?" My Mother asked.

"He drives a city garbage truck. Has for the past twenty some years." I know she did that for the knock-me-out-effect it had on both of them who probably dreamed I was going with a girl whose Dad was an investment banker. If I wasn't so sad and mad that they were giving her the 'twenty questions' drill, I might have laughed.

Grandmother leaned forward in her chair. "Is the same thing true of your hair that is of your dress?"

"To some extent."

Grandmother's gaze seemed to narrow. "I thought only colored women and those ones from Africa wore their hair like that?"

"And even some Mexican women," Lor said.

The look on my Grandmother's face was surprised shock. "I thought those Spanish ones always wore it combed up or combed long."

"Times change, Mother," my Mother interjected, again. "Dinner should be ready. Let's go in."

That was probably the first and last time I would know of that my Mother saved the day. Jeaninne, the cleaning lady who sometimes cooked, served us a wonderful meal of fried chicken, mashed potatoes, green beans, biscuits and gravy. It didn't necessarily go down well, worrying when the next bomb shell would be dropped on Lor, but it was delicious. All through it, Lor was the picture of poise and grace. Not once did she respond in anger to my Grandmother's continued SS probe. By the end of the meal, I had had all I could take, but there was desert and coffee on the patio. After we finished, Lor took out a Camel and seeing no ashtray, was about to put it away when my Mother found one and she lit it.

My Grandmother's comment seemed so weird and out of place that it resembled an 8.0 earthquake, as it started slow, and then spilled all over the patio. "None of my girls smoke," she exclaimed with a look of subtle distain at both of us.

"I smoke very little, Mrs. Feit," was Lor's reply and I was up out of the chair like a shot, almost knocking it over.

I made the excuse that we'd found a motel because we didn't want to disturb them. I hoped it was the last time I would have to lie. We said our 'thanks and goodnights' and were out the door, promising to see them Sunday after their church. When we got in the car I drove slowly away until the corner and then turned and gunned it out of there. Lor looked at me and tried to laugh, but she couldn't disguise the tears and I gave her my handkerchief.

"Where are we going?"

"I think you can guess."

"We wound through the San Fernando Valley freeways, picked up the Grapevine and began to relax a little once we got over the top and up past Bakersfield. A marathon day at the wheel. I figured we'd be home by midnight. The next day I'd call and tell my Mother we'd come home because Lor didn't feel well. Screaming with anger would have accomplished nothing. Even I was wise enough to know that. It wasn't very dramatic, but I knew my childhood had ended. Lor leaned into me and finally fell asleep. We made good time and pulled into our place around twelve-thirty. We would talk about it tomorrow.

chapter twenty-six

"I'm sorry for taking you down there." I was sitting on the couch and Lor was making coffee in the kitchen. "I didn't have to go. They are a couple of grade-A assholes. I hope that didn't hurt you down deep somewhere." She came into the living room, handed me a cup and sat down. "God, from all I've told you, you know I don't have any hidden feelings of loyalty."

"I called my Mom when you were in the shower. They definitely want us this afternoon for a BBQ and a talk."

"Man, you got the luck of the draw. They're not just on your side but on ours."

"I know. Guess I've always taken it for granted. I don't know how you grew up with that torture without leaving."

"Never entered my head cause' I had zero awareness. Just figured that's how everybody else lived."

"Thanks for getting me out of there." She hesitated. "Though it has its sadness, doesn't it?"

"How many times have I wondered aloud to you what it would have been like if my Mother and I had just been alone?"

"I don't know what to say, Mark. I guess we'll always be only a partial family." I waved my hand to indicate I didn't have anything to say either. The deed was done. To pass the time, we picked up and cleaned up before heading over to the city and her folks.

Sunday traffic was light since a rain had come in from the north. It was an easy and soothing rain, steady but slow as we crossed the Oakland Bay Bridge into San Francisco. Even though the summer hadn't ended, the traffic toward the ocean and her folk's place was just as light. We turned into the driveway and parked.

They opened the door before we could knock and gave us both a long embrace. It was obvious where Lor got her hugging from. I felt a warmth break through, and a few tears dropped down my cheeks as we went to the living room. I had agreed to let Lor tell the story of our crusade south.

"We want to hear all the details that you want to share." Mallie was sitting next to Lor on the couch. It was turning into autumn and a mellow but slightly cool breeze came into the room from the open kitchen windows.

Lor laughed, shook her head and looked at me. "I don't think we ever got as far as 'details' as far as I remember it."

"No details," I nodded and tried to put up a decent smile.

"But you must remember a couple of details?" Mallie insisted.

"Okay, I do. They wanted to know what Dad did and when they learned it was garbage collection both of their eyebrows practically leaped into their hairlines." Jack's mouth dropped a little but turned into a smile. "And then there was my smoking and hair. They called it 'colored' hair. Am I really that dark skinned?" She gave her laugh that sounds like a grunt. This made Mallie laugh too. "I had a single cigarette after dinner and dear old grannie looked rather sternly at me and said, 'None of my girls smoke.' But the dinner was good and the drive back, long. How about you Markie?"

"A good summing up except you forgot the separate bedrooms if we'd stayed overnight."

"I doubt if they're in touch with the new world. You guys gotta' forgive them that." Jack said.

"I agree," Mallie confirmed. "But you two were nice?"

Lor wrinkled her nose at her Mother. "We were the essence of niceness. You know that." Mallie shook her head and patted Lor's arm. "But the really hard part we haven't talked about yet. Can you guys imagine what little Mark lived through?" Mallie came over and sat next to me.

"Having to go through all the guilt laid on him. No real emotion towards him, no love, and I can guarantee you that those two are the pinnacle of emotionlessness. I couldn't believe it."

Jack looked at me for a long time before he spoke. "But how could that be?" It wasn't a made-up question. He honestly didn't know.

"And then I felt what he must have over the years and didn't think anything was wrong: the guilt manipulation. It hit me hardest when his grandmother laid the 'none of my girls' on me along with the 'colored' hairdo thing. For me, it was this sickening slam in the face, but it passed right over Mark because he didn't know."

"I thought everybody lived like that."

Mallie leaned over and kissed my cheek. "It must have been awful."

I looked at her and smiled. "Like Lor said, I didn't know."

"So, what's the conclusion to all of this?" Jack asked.

I shrugged my shoulders and held out my hands, palms up in resignation.

Mallie squeezed my hand.

"I guess we're half a family. But that's really better than none and we wouldn't expose you two to them under any circumstances." She hesitated. "Short of marriage, I guess." Lor glanced at me for confirmation and I gave it with my eyes.

Jack smiled and leaned forward in his chair. "I'd like to speak about a delicate subject since we're talking that way." Mallie was about to raise her hand but stopped. Jack leaned back deep in the chair as he spoke. "I can't help wondering about you two." He glanced at us both.

"I'm in my senior year, and Mark has acceptance into the Ph.D. program next semester but will only take a couple of classes since we need his PO job along with my math tutoring. That's about it. Honestly, I don't think either of us have a clue."

"I don't mean to be pressing you." Jack said. "So, for now, all is status quo?"

"Don't worry, Jack, we won't run off and not tell you folks. You know we're in love and we love you both for your support." I reassured them, not that they needed it.

"Now that we're on the subject," Mallie hesitated. "I know Lor will kill me but, damn it, you two have been together for some time. Where's this all headed?"

"Well, I'm having his child in a few months. Surprise!" Lor joked.

"Come on, Taylor. Give us a break." Mallie always called her 'Taylor' when she was super serious.

Lor glanced at me with a big smile as if she'd just done something very clever. "We haven't gotten into that yet, but I think this semester we'll be talking about it more."

"Good, that's enough for me to know. You two will bring up the subject next time." Mallie said.

"Do you two think he's gonna be a pretty good catch? Make lots of money and all that?" Lor was trying to lighten the mood.

"You know we're just concerned about you two?" Jack interjected. We both nodded and Mallie called for dinner as if the subject had temporarily ended. I loved them even more, or what I thought was love, by the time we left. It was hard to know what it really was.

chapter twenty-seven

Lor and I got deeply into school that first semester of her senior year, and I found more reluctance to beginning the Ph.D. At first, I wouldn't admit it for fear of not really knowing what to do. I also sent in the Lookout Application to the Forest Service in Oregon which wouldn't start until early June when Lor graduated. She was overjoyed that she would be included as part of the Lookout team with me, assuming I got lucky as hell and they accepted me.

She insisted in both Spanish and continued Math, and though I was resistant to both, I was very touched by her concern that I learn them. We had our weekly routines which included dinner and listening to Jazz in the city on Fridays and Sunday dinner with Mallie and Jack.

Sometimes we'd get together with friends from school who were usually in English grad school or Math. As you can imagine, those parties made for an interesting combination of ideas since Lor was reading the books I read, and she astounded the English contingent with her knowledge way beyond math. There was always a little marijuana floating around, but nobody could afford coke so that was one less worry for me. The fall semester was the best I'd known in college because I wasn't in school, even if I was going into a program I wasn't sure of. It was Lor who really made it 'best' for me. We divided the chores and seldom argued. And if we did argue, the silence never lasted more than a minute—a trait she'd learned from Mallie and Jack. And, not to forget, our making love became so trusting and relaxed that by winter break she could almost make love in the light. I can't tell you what a treat that was for me. Lust had rapidly faded and was more and more becoming love.

Yet by semester break, I sensed a very delicate change in her. It was so subtle I didn't even believe it was there at first. It was Mallie who took me aside one Sunday and pointed it out.

"You're not wrong, Mark. Jack and I have noticed too."

"So, what can we do?"

There was a hint of pain across her face. She shook her head in frustration. "That's just it, we don't know. When she's been like this before we tried talking, but she'd say everything was hunky-dory."

"Maybe it's just Christmas approaching?"

Mallie shook her head again. "She's always fine around the holidays. It's never then that something happens. Plus, you two are very happy together, right?"

"Yes, God yes…very happy. Mallie, what I've never understood is how she can have such loving and understanding parents, as I'm sure you've always been, yet she still has this drug thing around the edges of our lives. I mean we've talked a lot about the rape and this older guy from Jack's work who really made a hurtful impression on her. I think we're close enough that when she says those experiences haven't disabled her, I really believe she's straight with me. But I've still got that nagging doubt."

"Trust yourself, Mark. Nobody's been as close as you. Maybe, including us, I think. Sometimes I think we all could be tougher on her, you included."

"You know me, I'm sure the scars of my family, if you can call it that, still make me a person who thinks punishment is a loving gesture; at least how I got attention and, damn it, didn't even know it and still keep doing it. And guilt tripping myself all the time. Maybe my wanting to have her care for me has been too much understanding, too much pleasing. I don't know up from down, Mallie. I only want her to come back and stop slipping. She's too beautiful for any more hell. All I think of is caring for her."

Mallie squeezed my arm affectionately. "Jack and I are so happy about that. I know you have a hard time accepting compliments, but you have to start, no matter how hard. Don't you know how happy she's been since you two got together? Even her friends say that. That's a big thing, Mark. And look at yourself. You came back and returned to school and are almost on your way to graduate school. And don't forget the work you do in a week."

Now I shook my head. "Yeah, but don't you see, nobody gave me the encouragement to take a compliment in!

It's like water off a duck's back. I just haven't learned to take it in."

Jack called down to us in the yard that dinner was ready. "So, I think Lor and I may be alike, sort of, in that way but you two were and are so full of love for her. What in her past could have gotten her into these weird moods, almost like my guilt syndrome? A different kind of despair."

"Weird and dangerous," Mallie interrupted. She hugged me.

"I'm always trying to clear these subconscious tapes in my head. I do keep trying. Maybe she is too in her own way." She took my arm and we climbed the stairs to the kitchen.

chapter twenty-eight

I held my conversation with Mallie in the back of my mind. It wouldn't let go as we seemed to crawl into the fall semester. Lor's spirits were up some even though January, February and March were heavy with grey clouds and rain. That's not to say she didn't have her down moments, but these would rise and fall and didn't hang on.

Both of us had gotten a raise and, not being heavy consumers, our bank account continued to grow. Other than Dave and Annie and the people from her old house, we were amazingly content just being with each other, under the quilt and out. Yet even with her mood swings, her body hang-up was fading away almost naturally for reasons I didn't want to admit to being true because they were so good. I really believed I had won a whole lot of her trust and I was beginning to think somebody—Lor—really loved me. It was less like water off a duck's back; I could sometimes really feel it expanding inside.

I would say all that rain bought the curse of mathematics back into my life because she had pushed me through Advanced Algebra onto the outskirts of Calculus. It had returned as a ritual. I knew I'd never be a wizard, but I especially liked the horseplay mixed in with it. Yet I think we both liked the breaks we would take from studies and math when the sky would patch out with streaks of sun mixed across white-grey clouds and some cold but tolerable wind. We'd usually hike to the high park on our north side of campus and sit on a special log, warm in our down jackets and ski hats, and drink some espresso mixed with bourbon. The conversations were mostly silence since we were together so much now, but they would eventually drift around to the main topic: us.

She poured out some liquid into a shared thermos cup, then studied me and looked down at the log. "What exactly are you feeling?"

"I'm feeling like a math prodigy since I'm being tutored by a genius."

"Come on!"

"I think you know what I'm feeling for a while." I sipped the hot liquid.

"You're worried about me."

I moved over and sat close to her. "Yeah. You've been up and down this winter. I worry. To be honest, your Mom and Dad worry too." I bent over and kissed her ear that was sticking out between corn rows. "You mean too much to all of us, and especially to me. You get it."

"Yes, you know I do." Lor grabbed my hands and held them tightly. "And yes, I have been moody. Okay, look, I know you won't understand fully. Nor will they. But I still have my moments of being pulled in. Of being helpless. The rehab always tells you that you'll have it, the urge, for life, but you have to do the 'one day at a time' bit." She held and kind of shook my hands up and down. So, when I'm tired or down, I'm just hanging on sometimes."

"But you get tons of love, sweetheart. How does that get swept aside? If I could have had a few ounces of that growing up, I'd have given anything. You lived in an emotional oasis. I lived in a desert. Why can it still hang on? What's holding it in place?" Lor kept hold of my hands and looked out toward the wet grass and trees. She said nothing for several minutes. I could hear the wind rising and falling in cycles and was ready to say something myself.

"After the childhood I had compared to yours, you'll think I'm an ungrateful bitch."

"What?"

"I'll bet you've been searching your whole life, without ever realizing it, for some meaning in it because you never had a family that helped give it meaning. And I've had all the things you've longed for, and *still* tried to escape it with the damn drugs." She got up and walked down in the wet grass. I was going to follow but she turned, came back and sat down again. "You agree?"

"Yes, sure."

"I thought I got through the rape okay. And that older guy too. It isn't that. It's sometimes this feeling comes over me from *nowhere*, that nothing really has any meaning at all. Like we're just dropped here, live a while, and die.

Nothing! And it doesn't matter how much love there is because it's all gonna die in a good or bad time, no matter what." She took my hands again. There were a few tears down her cheeks. "There. I told you. I've never told Jack or Mallie. Nobody but you."

Lor's hands fell away from mine but I grabbed them and pulled her up off the log. We hugged, rocking back and forth for several minutes, our cheeks gently touching. "That must be an awful feeling."

"It's shitty." We sat back down and poured out the rest of the hot drink. "That's when the drug thing comes in. I've thought and thought about it but can't come up with a source that brings it on. It started when I was in junior high school."

"And you've held it in all this time? My God!"

"But I'd say that I've mostly been positive, don't you think?"

"Yeah," I smiled, "Positive…. and sometimes a little nutso. That's a compliment!"

"This time together, I've been really happy." She kissed my day's growth of beard on the chin.

"God, yes. Very, very happy. The best of my life so far, Lor, honest." The wind had risen.

We walked down through the park and residential streets to our house. It was cool inside, so I lit a fire and we settled on the couch. It was almost twilight. "I know you think my own search gets me off track sometimes, but I want to share something that dovetails in on what you just said in the park." She didn't comment which meant she was receptive. "You know that Gary Snyder and a few others have opened a whole new world for me where spirit and the out of doors blend? Well, he's also been a stepping stone into Buddhism and Zen. I've been reading a lot. Our meditation is part of that. And I guess some of it gets by me, too subtle. But they, the Buddha, talk about living and dying to each moment; a total presence second to second. He also said life wasn't permanent. It depressed the hell out of me and still does, even after a dozen readings of the same stuff. I still can't sit more than a second or two without some thought bombarding me. I think my depression may be a lot like yours: life then death and fertilizer again."

"Everything. Dreams and all meaningless and, as you said, impermanent."

I nodded. "But a little light is breaking through for me. The Buddha says there is no life and no death, and I don't get that yet, even intellectually, but he also says that everything is connected. In other words, we're all one. I know that's a tough one because that means even bad people are part of us. That, at least, I can understand intellectually. That's at least something. And I can't shake this Greek poet Seferis who says, '.... *like the branches of a terrible willow tree heaped in unremitting despair.*' If I understand you at

230

all, I can see you as a beautiful white-blonde-haired willow sometimes bent in the worse kind of despair."

"I never thought of that, me as a willow but the 'unremitting despair' is like what I feel when those moods on life and death come." She almost squealed in realization as she threw herself over me and bit my nose. "So, two of us can honestly feel it." She slid down and lay staring at the fire. Right now, it seemed we'd talked ourselves out but maybe we'd stumbled into an open doorway.

chapter twenty-nine

By late March we were still in an El Nino rainy weather pattern, but now when the rain came it was more forgiving, falling lightly for hours. Lor had christened it 'God rain." So far, she hadn't slipped so I hoped all the talk we'd been doing about 'despair' and the life and death thing, our impermanence, were getting us to at least being able to stare it in the face.

That week I knew she was happy although I was less so because I'd been fully accepted into the Ph.D.. English program with a teaching fellowship and she into the Master's program in Math. We spent money we didn't have and went with Mallie and Jack to Ernie's in the city. My celebrating was mostly on the surface because what I had come to see as the backbiting and stupidity of the academic world was wearing on me. There was so much politics and bullshit posturing. It didn't seem to faze Lor, probably because she was the number one choice for her graduate program. We incessantly teased Jack at dinner because he had insisted she learn it. His retort was that she could now be a math scholar who also spoke fluent Spanish.

The rain just kept coming as we moved into April. When I got the notice of employment as a lookout in Oregon near the Crater Lake area, I was surprised at how elated I was. It was a sudden release from a direction I wasn't all that keen on going in. I think Lor was happier for me since the program allowed for bringing your wife which we put in quotes (lied!) on the application because it gave us time to spend a whole summer alone. It also eased that recess of darkness in my mind about her falling away, a fear I had not done a good job putting aside. Fortunately, we could be in Oregon the second week of May to begin the season. We were driving the trusty old Volvo, so there'd be plenty of room for books and yoga mats, a practice we'd started together last semester. She loved puzzles. She said they were like a meditation, so we'd gotten a puzzle board and she'd take about ten 1000-piece designs. She had even started to feed us in line with how we'd eat at the lookout.

I was able to get time away from my PO job which had taken on a life of its own, which included a promotion that could turn into a full time fall back job if I wanted it when I returned. Dave and Annie had a couple they knew from L.A. that would sublet our place for the summer through early September, and Paul had agreed after Annie personally told him she would take full responsibility if they caused a problem.

chapter thirty

Finally, in the second week of the month the rain disappeared, and the skies were clear and warm. On Tuesday, Mallie and Lor made a date for lunch at a new place Mallie and Jack had found on Union Street overlooking the Marina harbor. It was Mallie's birthday and they'd traditionally spent it together—no men. It included shopping afterwards, so I expected her home easily by the time I got off my PO shift at nine.

When I got home it was dark outside and there were no lights on inside. I figured Lor had been tired from the long day and went to bed early. But we always left a light on for the other if we were the last home. I quietly let myself in, took off my coat and went down the short hall to the bedroom. Inching the door open softly, I worried she'd hear since she slept lighter than me. The light from the living room reflected through the crack in the bedroom door. I almost tripped on the rug when I realized that she wasn't there.

A dozen visions piled up in my head as I ran to the kitchen and out the door to the garage; the Volvo wasn't back yet. Was she in an accident? Abducted? Just late because they had a good time? The first and second visions were too horrible to think about. I grabbed the phone and called Jack and Mallie. It seemed forever until it was answered. Jack sounded cheerful enough.

"Where's Mallie, Jack?"

"She's right here." Suddenly he wasn't so cheerful. "Why?"

"Lor isn't home yet, Jack. Did they stay out later than expected?"

"Na....no.... Mallie has been back four, five hours. Oh, my God!"

Mallie was on the phone now. "Mark.... where is she?"

I was almost crying, "God, I don't know Mallie. She just isn't here. That's five hours since she left you!"

"Have you called the police?"

"I'll call them when I hang up. Usually they say at least 24 hours for declaring a missing person. Let me call them anyway. I don't know what else to do, Mallie."

"We don't either. Oh, God. Call back as soon as you can and let us know what they say."

"I will...I will." I hung up and dialed 911 and the dispatcher put me through to the Oakland Police. I shouted into the phone that I lived in Berkeley, but she was off the line. It seemed like an hour before the police answered. I told them where I lived, and they said they covered Berkeley off campus. The sergeant was polite and took a description and told me about the 24 hours and then they'd ask for a picture.

He took my number and that of her parents and said he'd call if anything developed. Christ, what a feeling of helplessness! I looked across the kitchen counter and out the living room into the darkness. I called Mallie and Jack and told them. I didn't know what to do when I put the phone down. I lit a fire and stared at the flames.

About an hour passed and the phone rang. I raced to the kitchen to get it.

"Hi." It was Lor. She sounded ok.

"Where the hell are you? You've had us worried sick."

"I drove down to the cabins. I just wanted some time alone."

"Jesus, couldn't you have told your Mom or called me at work? Do you know what it's like to come home and find the person you love most in the world not there?"

"I'm sorry. Please forgive me. I just felt so good after Mom's birthday and all. It was thoughtless of me. Completely. I didn't mean to worry you guys."

"You'll be back tomorrow morning?"

"I absolutely promise. They even had me for dinner and gave me our cabin."

"I won't sleep tonight, Lor."

"I won't either after this monstrous inconsideration. I'll call Mom and Dad and reassure them. I'll be home bright and early. I'm safe here. You know that."

"Okay, but no detours."

"I won't. I love you." She hung up before I could say it back to her. I mixed myself a double bourbon and tried to calm myself. But I couldn't. I immediately called Manford, hoping he would still be at the store. He answered and had a way of making it sound tolerable.

The drink took hold quickly, but I almost jumped when the phone rang again, and it was Jack.

"She sound ok to you, Mark?"

"I think so. Called down to the cabins and talked to the owner. Said she had dinner with him and his wife. Said she seemed fine."

"I hope so."

"Me too, Jack." We hung up and I called the police to tell them that we found her.

I drove over that night and stayed with them, sleeping in Lor's old room. I don't think my eyes closed once all night. I heard Jack up at five and joined him for coffee. There wasn't much to express except our worry about what might be the outcome. I called Manford about eight and he said he'd keep an eye out for her.

Every time the phone rang, either Jack, Mallie or I could feel its sound grating into us. Manford called back and said she hadn't come out yet. We urged him to check on her right away.

He called back fifteen minutes later. His voice was breaking up, but he sounded like he was trying to control it. "She didn't answer so I let myself in. She looked asleep but then I noticed what looked like drug stuff on the coffee table next to a bottle of wine she bought last night. I came around the couch and touched her shoulder. She half opened her eyes, then closed them. I knew something was off, but I didn't want to leave her. Irene was out front of the store and I motioned for her to call 911. She's still on the phone with them and said they would be here in about five more minutes from the Big Sur Fire-Rescue station. I'm waiting here until they come. She's still alive, thank God! I'll call you as soon as they get here and examine her. She's alive. Remember that."

We stood in the middle of the mid-morning kitchen, sun falling around us, just looking at each other, not knowing what to do. We were like statues; our eyes talking to each other. It was ten minutes later when Manford called back. He immediately put the paramedic on the phone with Jack. You could see the strain on his face as he listened. He sighed and thanked the paramedic and said we were on our way down there.

Mallie ran over to him. "He said they had her stabilized and were heading up to Carmel Valley Hospital. He warned me that this was the early stage so be prepared. Lord," Jack said as he looked up into the kitchen sunlight as if he was speaking to it. "Taylor, my sweet baby, what the hell have you done?" Then he turned and hugged Mallie. I joined them.

He drove like a man possessed and we made good time, getting there about noon. Lor was in intensive care and only family could go there. I waited on a plastic chair in the hall until I saw them come out, shake hands with the doctor and come towards me. I practically ran to them. They gathered me in with a hug, a hug like I'd never known until them and Lor.

They both looked exhausted even though it had been only a few hours. Jack spoke first.

"The doctor said the dose was big. He didn't know how she'd survive it. She's just out of the critical stage so they're moving her to UC Medical Center about two. We can ride along in the ambulance, but you'll have to drive the car, Mark. UC is better equipped to care for her and they have a built-in rehab facility."

"We're sorry you can't go with us," Mallie said.

"I understand. But what did the doctor say?"

"She looks very tired. He said it looks like she'll make it, but it'll take a week or so at UC before they can say for sure. And then there's got to be months of rehab."

"A week!" I almost shouted it out. Mallie took my hands.

"They always say that, Mark. But then it will be months."

Jack cut in, "They also said if she ever did this again with the amount she ingested, the outcome would be much bleaker."

"So, what do we do now? It's two hours before the ambulance leaves."

"The doctor said we should get something to eat and be back here a little before two."

chapter thirty-one

I couldn't keep up with the ambulance and it took me a while to find them in the gigantic UC Med Center. As a precaution, they would keep her in Intensive Care for a couple of days until they were sure she was stabilized. The same rule unfortunately applied there; only immediate family.

Her parents were so loving and sympathetic with me that I felt like their son-in-law. I asked if I could do anything, but they sent me home and would call a couple times a day and let me know her progress and when I could see her.

Thinking of her every day did two things to me. First, I had very little focus even though I somehow managed to go to the PO and get my work done. But not at the level of before Lor's drug situation. Second, I was totally surprised by my other reaction: I was getting angrier by the day and feeling progressively more disgusted with the whole scene. As guilty as it made me feel, I was beginning to feel like some chess piece that was being moved around for her convenience. I waited until Lor was stable and her parents were a little calmer before I offered to take them to dinner. We met on a Saturday night before the crowd scene at most restaurants. It was Chong's Chinese in the basement of a

building on Jackson and was nearly empty when we settled
into a booth. They didn't look terrific, but better.

"How are you holding together, Mark?" Mallie
asked.

"To be honest?"

"Of course, you are family," Jack affirmed.

"Well maybe this is too honest."

"No. Tell us."

The waiter interrupted us with the usual insults
Chong's was famous for and we asked for our beers before
the food. Yet another insult before he left that at least made
us smile.

"Remember, you guys asked me." They nodded.
"Okay. She's with me all the time. It's hard to get my mind
off her and her condition but I'm making it through."

"We withdrew her from the Master's program for
medical reasons, obviously. But she can finish next year,"
Mallie said hopefully.

"I know. She really has only 6 units to finish. But
the more she's on my mind, the guiltier I feel about being
angry with her." The waiter bought our beer and we avoided
talking by examining the label and taking a sip. I suddenly
felt I shouldn't have entered this territory because I sensed it
was more dangerous for them than me. "This anger came out
of nowhere, I swear, but it's real and I can't avoid it, though
I'd like to because then the guilt would go away. How can I

love Lor and be angry with her? I feel both an anger and the *despair* of a great poet I know. And I know Lor felt."

Jack broke their silence. "Mark, let me say something that might make it easier for you to go forward." I waited. "We've agonized over what I think you're about to say."

"But Jack, isn't there a time you have to be tough? We all love her, but it seems there must be a time to be tough with Lor. I feel like I'm strung out in space, waiting in the wings for her to come around and the reason I'm angry is because there doesn't seem to be any reason someone who is loved as much as her can't get her act together. You must have those same feelings of wanting to get tough, telling her to cut the bullshit and get real. Hell, it seems she's gotten through the rape, and I know she's better about this older guy who treated her so lousy. What can it be, beyond that?" I was almost crying with the frustration and anger.

"I know Mallie and I are to blame for always giving her excuses, but we always forgive out of love and thinking what could happen if she went off the deep end because we were tough. We do hear you and understand. We've never understood why she would do this. We raised her with the same love we did all our kids and they're fine as far as we can tell."

"It's not that I love her any less, and God forbid if anything happened to her, but I'm at the point—probably for the first time in my life—that I'm consciously thinking of myself. And I don't want to live life pleasing others by letting them walk on me, with or without love. As you know, that's been the story of my life until now. I know she doesn't think that, but that's what it comes down to. What am I supposed to do, wait outside the hospital until she says I can come in? I have a life too. And so do both of you." I sat back and drank some beer, feeling hot all over. "I didn't mean to go on…"

Mallie interrupted, "No, it's good you did. You had the courage to air something that was kind of rotting in the dark. We should have bought it up, but it never seemed to be the right time, which is probably an excuse for avoiding it."

Jack asked, "What do you think it could be?"

"I don't know Jack except we've talked about being literally overcome by despair. We've both felt that—the meaningless of living. But I for sure know that I love her like I've never loved anyone. Hell, I didn't have any idea what love was until now! And I'm scared to death to lose her. But I can't live a life waiting in the wings, even if I love her. You know about the lookout job. I know she will be in the hospital and rehab for some time. Maybe it's better for me to go north and hope for the best. I realize that leaves you to figure out a way to work it out, but I have to go. And see what fate deals us."

It surprised me to see them almost smile. "We understand. And it is up to us to begin demanding a real return on our love for her, even if we must take the risk. I don't know what the source of this whole thing is, but we've met with the psychiatrist twice. She's with him an hour a day. We asked him the same question, and he says after seeing her that he can't get any information from her that would give him the answer to the source. But he does believe there is a source, even as normal as she appears to him right now. He's seen people like Lor before in his practice. We'll have more sessions and as she recovers, he wants us to meet with Lor and him. Believe us, Mark, you're not deserting her. There'll be plenty of time for you to get involved when you come back."

It was good I'd reached an understanding with them, but my despair went on, day after day. For the next month, I haunted the City Lights looking for a book that would answer it and picked up more books for my hours alone as a lookout. I got drunk and surprised Dave and Annie by smoking some weed with them. They didn't have any answers, but their sympathy helped some. I even walked up and down Broadway and Columbus looking for the druggy she'd seen because I hoped he'd be able to tell me something, but for all I know he was gone or dead.

Sometimes I couldn't sleep and walked the north side of campus up and through the park and back from the time the moon was up until it dropped into the west and the trees began opening to dawn. This must have gone on for at least three weeks into mid-May, but time had lost its linear quality—just rolling from light to dark, dark to light.

My awareness always seemed peripheral to whatever scene it was passing through until I would get a call from Jack or Mallie and they would tell me how she was. That would bring me back to the moment. They said she had wept a lot when she was told I was leaving, but still didn't want to face me. Though they said it was obvious that rejecting me had just been a momentary emotional, irrational part of her recovery. At moments like that, I fought the urge to drive to UC Med and break into her ward. But I forced myself to pack up the car for the trip north.

I had been given a leave of absence because the man who hired me juggled the books and made me full time to be eligible. I took my PO foul and cold weather gear and borrowed a warm sleeping bag from Dave. They'd said nothing about booze, so I brought enough to last three and a half months and conned myself into calling it a way to warm up on cold nights. I'd have to switch to bourbon and water but figured any port in a storm. Paul gave me more than enough room in the garage to store Lor's and my extra stuff. I hoped our sublet or another unit would be open when I returned. He assured me it would. My goodbye call to Mallie

and Jack was sad but clean. Mallie said Lor had asked for
me.

chapter thirty-two

It took me less time than I estimated, and I arrived at the Crater Lake Emergency Services Center about an hour early. I had tried to focus on the scenery, but Lor's smile kept appearing and the rolling hills of forest and highway seemed secondary. The Center was on a concrete drive. It was two-story with a long tin roofed and open garages on either side that must have housed at least fifty pieces of equipment from trucks, skip loaders and giant earth movers. There was a full-service bay where half a dozen machines were up on hoists being worked on.

I found the District Supervisor 1 who was my boss. Instead of going into his office, he took me out back to a grassy picnic area on a patio next to the glass-walled cafeteria, both of which looked out on a thick stand of trees. We sat on a bench there.

"Glad you made it in one piece, Mark." His opening remark gave me the feeling that he'd be good to work for, not like the government bureaucrat I'd expected. "I'd be repeating myself if I explained the job now since that's what we'll be doing part of the morning tomorrow. My only question now is, are you okay being alone since your wife couldn't make it? I ask because we have dropouts every year."

"I'm fine with that. Back in Berkeley before Taylor, my wife, (I lied) came into my life I was always seeking quiet spots to study or just read. I have no problem being alone. I just wish she could have come but we decided she'd stay home and help her mother. She hasn't been real sick but up and down, and Taylor wanted to be there for her."

"Well, from my viewpoint, it makes it easier to have just one person in a lookout. We've had marriages split up when the job is kind of shared. But we'll get into all that tomorrow. Right now, I'll show you where you'll bunk for the night. By the way, the cafeteria is open twenty-four hours a day." He smiled, "I think you'll like the food."

He showed me a garage where lookouts could leave their cars for the summer, then took me inside, introduced me all around to the regular crew, showed me the cafeteria and led me upstairs to an empty bed in the station's main sleeping area. It was approaching sunset, so I showered and went back down to dinner.

I felt welcome and blended in and felt like I was a seasoned veteran of fire and rescue. After dinner, we went outside and sat on the huge back porch facing the forest. We shot the breeze, smoked and drank a beer until the long road trip crept up on me and I headed up to bed. As I lay there, I felt like my world and Lor's were really separated. There was a tinge of longing and homesickness, but they were hard to hold onto at that distance and I fell quickly asleep with a mind at rest.

About nine, we had a general meeting of the lookouts and my boss. A few other official looking types sat in but didn't say much. The guys I'd be sharing radio contact with for the next three plus months were a mixed bag ranging from some leftover hippy looking guys with beards and long hair, to some super military looking guys with short hair and crisp looking green uniforms (optional).

My boss was very relaxed, very casual, but his talk with us made it obvious that what we were about to do was a serious matter. I took notes on how to operate the radio and other items about my tower that I thought would be useful. There would be an easy radio code book on sight that could be mastered in less than a half hour. In a day or two, those who hadn't done the job before would be up to speed.

We were allowed so much stuff of our own and the rest was supplies that would be hauled to our destination. After lunch, I met the fire and rescue team member who would escort me to my post, about five miles up country from the station and to the right of Crater Lake.

I helped him pack a mule and we set out on horseback about one. Bill Dawkins was his name. He'd been on the team for eight years and lived in a government house with his wife and two children down the road on the Forest Service compound. It was a real community.

"Yeah, I know these closed communities where everyone works together and lives on a compound sounds like a recipe where guys are sleeping with other guys wives and there's a lot of bickering and gossip and just plain bullshit, but it's surprising how little we see each other off duty. Oh, sure, some people are closer than others and some of what I mentioned does go on. But overall, things are pretty straight. And if anyone throws the balance off, they usually get discovered and shipped out. A few have even been fired in my time. Overall it's mellow." We were riding up through a dry river bed with the midday sun coming straight down onto the forest floor. The horses and pack mule handled the rocky surface with ease. "What got you to apply for this kind of work, Mark?"

"This may sound a little strange, but it was a poet."

Bill laughed. "And his name by chance wasn't Gary Snyder?"

"How'd you know that?"

"Maybe a half dozen new guys have told me that. But you can feel right at home. I was one of those guys eight years ago!"

When we got there, we unloaded everything into a downstairs room which contained a small electric oven and refrigerator and water heater plus a sink and small table to prepare food on. There was even a toaster. "As you can see, this will be pretty much a canned food summer," Bill laughed, "but I come up about every three weeks with some meat or fish and salad fixings. So, if you're the healthy type it won't be that bad. Just a warning, power lines do come down, but you can always reach us on your radio. Also, the shitter is outside, and the shower will give you a short few moments of getting clean, though you probably won't get very dirty."

The stairway was the corkscrew type you found in fire stations and upstairs was a bunk, a desk looking out on the perimeters of my area of forest and a comfortable chair. The idea was I could read and watch at the same time. "Sorry about no music but there are some news channels out of Portland you can sometimes pick up. Naturally, no television."

"I'm happy for that," I offered. We spent about an hour of orientation, mostly reading the maps next to the desk you could scoot your chair over to, plus practice with the base on using the radio.

"You'll have the signals down in no time, don't worry. Believe me, there have been a lot of non-college graduates come through here."

"That's a relief."

"Don't sweat it. We all do but then it does come easy." Bill smiled. "Okay, I'll see you in about three weeks, barring bad weather which will happen sometimes." We shook hands and he disappeared down the stairs.

chapter thirty-three

He explored the lookout, top to bottom, including the outhouse which was plastic with an open trench whose odors had been quieted over the winter by lime. He also arranged his food neatly and unpacked, including the three quarts of bourbon that he hoped would last until the end of September. Then he arranged his living area, laid out Dave's sleeping bag and put his flashlight and batteries on a shelf next to the bunk. Last, he arranged the desk area, complete with writing pad and pen and pencils along with the lamp lighting the desk and chair. His final task was putting some stationery in the desk drawer with some stamps and envelopes.

It was nearing twilight and he sat on a log that had been crudely carved into a two-seated side-by-side chair looking partially north to the crater. It was warm enough in the light breeze and he sat there thinking about himself and Lor and the future. When he finally got up, he went straight to bed even though he wasn't all that tired. Lying there completely still, he thought he could feel the immense silence around him in the dark. After an hour, he got up with the flashlight and went to the desk. He leaned it on the desk so its light spread over the writing pad. He only wrote, "Mark Eliot, what the hell are you doing?"

Lor was in her fourth week of rehab. Nobody would tell her how long it would be until she went home. She didn't want to be in rehab. She didn't want to go home. Mark was somewhere out on the edge of the world. She couldn't find him. Couldn't even hardly imagine him.

She had just finished her session with the 'psychoman' as she called him. An hour and a half every day; it was so boring, boring. What was he trying to dig out of her? She couldn't find that either, no matter how hard she tried. She wore her short shorts almost every day with a wool sweater. He kept sneaking peeks at her legs, it was so obvious. He's probably ask her someday to take off her sweater. Keep your mind on your job, Bozo!

It was July now and Mallie and Jack had been to three sessions with her. They looked okay, but she felt so guilty about the money. Jack had wanted to retire in a few years. How could he do that with her screwing up again? She wanted Mark to come and hold her. They'd bought his picture in the first week. It was on the table next to her small bed in the room she shared with Beth, a meth freak, but nice to talk to sometimes or to listen to about Beth's addiction. He wouldn't want her back even if they said he did, even though they said he still loved her.

She was sitting in the perfect garden behind the buildings next to the koi pond. She liked the big goldfish more. She saw Beth come out of the counseling center and motioned to her. Even lunch was a treat when you had nothing else to do.

Beth kind of plopped down next to her and threw her head back with a sigh. She turned and looked at Lor. "Don't tell me—Bozo is eyefucking you again? Between that and looking for this mysterious source in us, don't they have anything better to do?" Lor only nodded. "Come on, let's go to lunch."

Afterwards they lay on their beds for a while until Mallie and Jack would come on his lunchbreak. "What'd he try this time?

"Just more talk about my childhood. He doesn't seem to get it. I had a wonderful childhood. There're no hidden closets or meanings; they straight out loved me and cared for me. I can say that with authority 'cause I know what Mark went through. The question still is why I am here and not him?" She turned in the bed and faced her. Beth lit one more off the chain she smoked in a 'no smoking room.'

"I see us as two girls who they think are pregnant but aren't. We just can't produce for them. We don't have a clue what it is, what they want from us." Beth held the inhale as if the cigarette was laced with weed. She got up abruptly and left, knowing Mallie and Jack were coming.

And they did in about ten minutes. She loved their coming and always began the conversation the same way

255

after the hugs and kisses. "I should be able to get out soon. I'm really feeling great."

"Taylor, you need to stay as long as they say."

"Why, they're not the authority on me. And it's costing you a fortune which adds daily to my guilt."

They were sitting in the garden in the same place she'd been. Jack touched her arm. "We'll get through that, Taylor." She loved him more, coming in his garbage collectors uniform.

"No, you won't. With the debt you can't retire, and I don't want that."

"Well, it is a debt that goes up," he admitted. "We just can't afford this fancy place again, but we want you to have the best."

"Sweetie, he's full of it," Mallie said. "We are getting to that point and he knows it. And he knows we can't go on much longer or we're in trouble over his pension."

After they had left she sat in silence. She fully knew she'd be a gutter junkie without their help, and she knew she didn't want that, but she hadn't got there yet. But what of Mark? Had he given up on her? He would if she told him the truth.

chapter thirty-four

Within a week, he had a routine that would stay with him for the summer until the job was finished in early October. He swept and mopped and dusted every day because the broad swing out windows to the north and east bought dusty winds almost every night. Well-placed maps would be blown around even though he held them down with books.

He'd check in with the dispatcher back at the station around eight to give him a "five by five, 10-4" which he would call in every four hours, rain or shine. It was mostly rain—more than they'd had in years—through early August when it tapered off to every other day or so until mid-September when Lor was supposed to be released and come home. Mallie had told him she was still afraid to call him because she felt it was over.

To avoid thinking about her, he immersed himself in a combination of novels, self-help and spiritual guide books and was reading as much as six hours during the day and before he slept. He usually was meditating an hour three times a day; the mantra he used changed every couple of weeks depending on what he was reading. But he noticed a subtle change in that his thoughts were quieting quicker and he didn't have to fight with them, rising and distracting him from what he wanted to believe was a real silence.

His communications were sparse with the other lookouts and at first that troubled him, but it became an effort to come up out of the silence which just wasn't like him. He was normally open and seeking friendship, but now he had grown at home with the world empty of people that surrounded him. His company were the few creatures of the forest who drank from the steam a hundred yards below him to the northeast. Most of them came two or three times a day, once around midday when he'd take his own lunch to the two-seated log and watch them, being careful not to spook anybody. The same ones came at the same time. Very few were large except for the occasional brown bears, often with cubs in tow. At night he often heard the rustle of bushes or sounds he couldn't identify.

He always took a nap after lunch. As soon as he closed his eyes, Lor's smile would appear even though he tried to let her face pass. All this bonding with the forest silence grew on him before he recognized and (almost unbelievingly) acknowledged it. It was just after dinner when her presence was the strongest, and he set as much time as needed to hold and play with their memories. That was the time Mallie and Jack would be patched over to him on the landline. He could count on them calling with their news every Sunday and Wednesday. They spoke tentatively about Lor, almost hesitant as if not wanting to disappoint him; she would tell them that she loved him. All summer it too became a mantra, "She loves you and…and she still can't speak because she feels so guilty about the whole thing." He'd protest every time, but they couldn't help though they tried so hard to smooth over his concern, assuring him she was looking great and doing well and would be home soon. They almost promised him she'd call. He'd hang up and feel the slow breeze until he got back to his reading and thinking.

It was an easy summer because of the strange rain pattern, but he welcomed the hours of contemplation and broke up all the thinking with walks down to the stream and back. At one point he noticed that the bourbon he sought and couldn't wait for at first had dropped off to one shot with some water before dinner, down from four shots at the beginning of the summer. He could never put a 'why?' to any of this. In fact, after so much intense reading, he didn't feel he had progressed much at all. But he did sense that all the self-help stuff he read only benefitted the authors since none of them really created pathways to answers. Yet the spiritual writings almost always had answers that opened pathways through dedicated practice. 'Aw, the hell with it. I doubt if I even believe that,' he thought.

A couple of weeks before his job finished, he got up one morning and stopped meditating, which he'd done religiously. He also stopped reading anything but his maps, which was a waste of time since rain had killed any summer possibility of fires. He did write a long heartfelt letter to Dino, but mostly stared into space and was up and down his corkscrew stairs and into the forest many more times than he had been before. He kept ending up on the two-seater log, staring up towards the crater or down through the trees toward the stream. Mark was becoming slowly depressed and wanted out. He was glad he'd tried but realized he was a different person than Gary Snyder.

I want to call him. But I can't. He doesn't care anymore. I'm sure. But how about you, stupid. You're the one who hasn't called him, you're to blame if he doesn't care anymore.

She had been home six days and slept late each day until the sun spread onto the bed through the shutters. She'd been welcomed back for the next spring semester, including her math scholarship. Lor should have been happy. But she wasn't. Her parents didn't bother her. Their lives went on without a hitch despite her long absence. They made her feel like she'd been away on a trip. Then, every day before getting up she would tense, and fear would come over her before she could try and stop it.

Mark would be home in two weeks. What were they going to do? He'd written one short note saying Paul had their old place available. Why did it scare her so much? She imagined them together again. She imagined how they made love. How tender it always was. Sitting in the park. How would any of it happen when they hadn't talked for months? She was a junkie. He couldn't expect to live with that threat anymore. Mallie and Jack had made that clear. They couldn't give up all they had left, Jack's pension, if it happened again.

How was she going to tell him what she'd always withheld? The shame and senselessness. How would Mallie and Jack take it? They didn't know either. They all said she got so much love from them and from Mark. *Then how could she 'junk-up' again she thought? Because I've never told them the truth, the whole thing, the despair, and, she thought, wouldn't withholding really be nothing but a rotten lie to people who've been so loving? I'm strong. But why couldn't I have been like that, then? I'm not really a druggie, no matter what I've called myself in at rehab. It's when this meaningless comes over me.* She was crying through her thoughts.

It was just days before he finished the lookout job and already he was half-packed and had cleaned the lookout well. He felt like there was nothing else he wanted to do. He hadn't been sleeping well, which was a new pattern for him since most of the summer he slept right through the night. Mark had tried going to bed later, but that didn't help. So, the last few nights he'd just lain there staring at the green painted wood ceiling. He stared at the ceiling again. It was lighter than last night and reflected the half-moon through the open windows.

Again, I felt so tired but couldn't sleep. But my mind wasn't like it had been. Now images of being a child seemed to begin like a movie against the green ceiling. Yet the first wasn't really an image. It was a feeling… A feeling like I couldn't move, couldn't breathe and I was short of breath for no reason. Then it disappeared as quick as it came, and there was my Dad and the girl with the dark hair on the path by the bungalows in Hollywood. Then it became me lying in the dark imagining the little dog they'd given me at the pet store but was now alone in the cold, dark garage beyond my window trying to get warm; I knew they never took him to a ranch. Were my eyes suddenly wet for that little dog or myself? Then came the aging Norwegian lady who held my hand above the flames, and my Mother's fear when the tree almost caught fire. I opened my eyes, but the images wouldn't stop. After my Dad died; the neighbor who helped me construct an electric train track on a table he built in our garage but had to stop until I went to the neighbor kid's house to apologize for hitting her boy after he'd started a fight, not me.

I got up in the moon darkness and poured a glass of the last bourbon and drunk it sitting on the bed, looking out at the tree shadows and mist. After feeling the cold, I got back into the bag and lay on my back on the thin cotton mattress. I remember a ride with my Dad to nowhere; I remember seeing the small bottle he kept in his door compartment. Then he was gone, and I saw my Grandmother's wrinkled face calling me "ya bum!" when I came home from an end-of-summer day at the beach.

The images wouldn't stop; as if creating themselves, they carried me where I had never realized before, to year upon year feeling the coldness of the house, seeing for the first time how truly separate in every way I had been from my Mother and Grandmother, carrying me to the end of high school, university and into the Army jail cell with Dino. Then it got faster as the first Jazz songs I heard carried into Kim's sweet face and the post office route through Berkeley and the psychic readings. Even in this semi-dream, I doubted what the psychic said about my home, that I'd never had a home. I opened my eyes and looked at the clock on the desk. It said three a.m. "The psychic couldn't have meant that." I said it twice, thinking of the horror of what she said, the poet's "unremitting despair" of it.

I drank another glass of bourbon in the desk chair and watched the moonlight as it passed over the lookout. "They couldn't have wished me dead?" I had asked that silently often, ever since the psychic told me two years ago. I remember smiling when I told Lor. She had cried softly and hugged me until my neck had gotten stiff and we had to shift positions in bed. Then I thought of all the books I had read since Dino, all the thoughts and experiences. What had it all meant? All the discussions I had with Dave and Annie and Lor and people I'd met on my route. What did it amount to? Why had I stopped meditating and, finally, reading?

I finished the dregs of the bourbon and got back into the bag very relaxed. When I closed my eyes, I fell asleep and didn't move until five. I heard an owl or another bird in the early dawn. I ate cereal and took a hot shower. Mornings were always cold there, even in summer, and I pulled on a Pendleton shirt and sweater and was warm again. There wasn't much left to cook, and I didn't feel like eating out of a can, so I made some coffee and went down in the first light to the carved log and sat overlooking the beginning sun spreading on the forest and river below me. It was as if the whole meaningless of my life had just passed in the dreams. I had never felt such lonely fear.

Beth was still asleep. I went down the hall to the cafeteria, got some coffee and carried it to a table. I was the only one there. One more day left, and I'd be out after a little over three and a half months plus so much guilt for putting them through it again. I got up and went to a full-length mirror by the door and pulled down my sweat pants and took of the sweatshirt. I just stared at myself. I looked normal enough and with a beautiful body that had survived it again. "Thank you" I said aloud and redressed and sat down at the table. *How can he keep loving me? Or has he stopped, and I don't know it? Does he feel like Mallie and Jack do? That I've reached the end of his sympathy too?* She glanced down at her arm. I really look beautiful. I'm not ashamed or feeling guilty for that. You couldn't see the needle marks unless you looked carefully: a lovely, white-pinkish, strong arm. Feminine yet built to lift and work. I have all this and I'm smart too, really smart. Mallie and Jack. And I'm caring. Mark says that so often. *Why didn't I write to him? Why did I refuse to see him before he left for the summer? Why did I junk out again?* It's like it comes for no reason but I know the reason: this 'unrelenting despair' that he quotes from the poet. He knows how it feels too. We're too young for such feelings. Our lives are barely awake. We shouldn't be stuck in these burdens. He'll be home from the woods soon. Paul is giving us our regular place back. *Will he come over first... and then in time take me home? Can I go, after this separation, or should we just end it?*

Lor went back to her room. Beth was still asleep. God, the stories she'd told: all the stealing and whoring and perversions for the smallest hit, anything for that. Even in sleep, Beth looked thirty, not twenty-two, a drawn out, gaunt twenty-two. And she was smart too. Why weren't they both smart enough? Did it truly drag you down without help for escape or ending?

Beth turned over, yawned and half smiled at Lor. "Taylor goes bye-bye today."

"Yeah," Lor half smiled too.

"Lady, don't be bleak for us on this day of redemption." She laughed.

"I won't."

Beth propped up her pillows and rested her head. "I'm ready for our last talk, our last mutual confessional."

"We're talked out, aren't we?"

"Yes, but I've got another two months they say. Whoever the hell 'they' is."

"I was just thinking about being out of here. Again."

"Don't be back, okay? Shoot yourself first but don't be back."

Lor nodded. "I was thinking maybe we're condemned to this push and pull forever. You've been in four times and me three. It's like there's no let go. At least that's what Dr. Psycho infers."

Beth messed with her hair, combing it back with her fingers. "He's full of shit and you're too smart not to know it. Plenty of people have made it. Hard, but made it." They pressed a "high five" on each other and Lor went to take hopefully her last shower in rehab.

I've been doing nothing but sit at the desk of maps as if they were not the outline of the forest beyond my broad

windows but of different planets. I arrange and rearrange
them as if I'm constructing a galaxy. Then I stare for
sometimes more than an hour out the window at the trees
and mountains and the changing shades of light as the day
progresses into twilight and beyond. I eat, use the portable
toilet, nap and regularly report in by radio. Or at least I know
I've done those things for the last six days. I even finished
my packing and I go back to headquarters tomorrow. Lor has
come and gone in my thoughts daily and stays for a while
when I look at the picture I have of us and her parents. Then
she fades but always returns. But never do I think beyond the
moment. Never about us and the future. Maybe I'm just a
coward.

     I can still feel what came fully six days ago as the
sun flowed brightly along the stream and down in shafts
through the trees. The animals had already taken their
morning water and there was nothing moving but the stream
below. When the light opened, the fear I had felt so intensely
faded, and that's when this past six days began. Even the
fear of disorientation I'd had all my life and its lack of
control didn't bother me when I came back to the lookout. I
had a hard time even figuring out where I was, but it was
okay until I did. I still don't understand whatever it was or is.
And that seems fine.

     Now it's time to go home. I've read enough books
for half a lifetime and meditated enough for two, yet the

need to read and meditate have slipped further away. I know she'll be back to haunt me as I drive out of this forest land into the sad mess of the world. My heart has finally come to say hello, to pull me away from figuring. I am saying for the first time, 'welcome,' and strangely letting it come. The experience was here and gone. But remains.

chapter thirty-five

Paul was in the garage when I pulled in the driveway on a cold, cloudy late afternoon after about eleven hours on the road. He waved and smiled and that was reassuring.

"You make decent time?"

"Yeah, really good. Traffic was light. It's great to see you. I'm glad to be back."

"Well, you're all set. My son and I moved your stuff back in and there's a fire ready to go."

He helped me unload the car and carry the stuff inside.

"About Lor...? I didn't want to ask, sorry."

"You're family, Paul. You know the story. I think she's out of rehab and home at her parents. We felt a reentry into our lives might work better if she stays there until she feels ready. She got her scholarship back for next spring." I heaved a sack with the leftover booze I'd forgotten onto the kitchen counter and took out the bourbon and mixed us a drink with water. We toasted but I could see in his expression that it wasn't anymore a toast for him than it was for me. "You both been doing okay?" I asked to shift away from the discomfort I felt.

"Yes, we're good. Good tenants all around and good health. Can't ask for more. Well, I'm gonna let you go and finished unpacking. You think you'll try for that doctorate program in literature again?"

I laughed. "You know, that's the first time I've thought about it all summer. I'm thinking about it second semester if the U lets me." I hesitated. "Thought we'd just feel our way for a while, no obligations but the PO. They're giving me the old job back with some extra days as a fill in if I want them."

"You going to be alright, financially?" He asked in a way that I knew what old Paul had in mind.

"You're such a good person, Paul. I saved all my money from the lookout. We'll be fine. I don't know if she'll want to go back to work right away as a tutor. I'm sure she'll feel like me; we want to help her Mom and Dad pay off what the insurance won't cover on the rehab debt."

He shook his head. "That's gotta be big. Okay, I'm out of here. Get some rest." He finished his drink and walked across the living room to the front door. He turned back. "Mind if I ask you something?"

"Like I said, you are family."

He paused for nearly a minute. "About Lor…. its been almost three and a half months…You gonna be okay?" He opened the door.

"I hope so. I really do hope so."

"We're here if you two need us, you know." He smiled and closed the door, not waiting for my reply. But I wasn't sure of anything suddenly. I really did hope so too.

All the time I was straightening and unpacking, I kept looking at the phone. I knew they'd picked her up a few days ago and they all knew I'd be getting home this evening. When I finished my work, I lit the fire Paul had laid, nuked a bean, cheese and rice microwave burrito I'd stopped for on the way home and opened a can of beer. It was then that I felt the pulling back into what our lives had been before I went to the forest, before the dawn, the sun and the stream, those moments that changed my life but I don't know how. It was like being pulled through a mirror; my body both relaxed and tensed. I sunk back into the chair and drank a third of the beer. I could feel the buzz rising inside. Then I put it down and stared at the fire.

My plan was to get tough up front with her. I couldn't be pushed and shoved even as much as I still wanted to be. The consequences would be what they'd be. But I had to be gentle too. I couldn't help it. I'd tell her straight out that I couldn't feel like the whipping boy anymore, always trying to adjust to her moods and ways. Mallie and Jack promised they'd be tough and they were through therapy and rehab. But it wasn't my nature. I'd been raised to be nice to guilt and punishment in hopes, I guess, that they would go away. That's what it all came down to as I sat there in this renewed reality.

I brought the phone to the couch and set it next to me. Finally, I picked it up and dialed. On the third ring, Jack picked it up and the first thing he said was, "She's in the shower. I'm doing a barbeque. How was the drive? Shut up, Jack! I'm sorry Mark but we've all been walking around on egg shells. She's fine. Go ahead and talk. I'm sorry."

"I've been sitting here an hour trying to get up the courage to call, so I know what you mean"

"Thank God for that, my friend."

"Tell me the truth, how's she doing? What's it been, four or five days?"

"Ah…seven…and we really can't believe she's adjusting so easily. Yesterday, she and Mallie went for lunch and some shopping. They came back happy, I think. But how about you?

"Believe me when I say it was an unbelievable summer in all ways."

"What do you think we should do?" He was back to Lor. "She's accepted the fact that we can't support this again, emotionally or otherwise. She really has. She seems different. I don't know if this is finally the end, but I think the talk therapy together was good. Mallie agrees. Mallie and I thought we'd disappear tomorrow and you could have the house to yourselves and then we'd come back for dinner."

272

"How does she feel about staying with you a while?"

"In truth, I really think from what she says she'd rather be with you, which is great from our point of view. How about you?"

I drank the rest of the beer. "You think we're up to that, so quick? We haven't talked in months since before she went in."

"I know but she talked a lot about you in most of the therapy sessions. She's still with you, even if you haven't been. You know what I mean?"

"I think so. But I'm not quite sure where I am, Jack. My love hasn't changed, but the mountains did something to me I can't define. It's not a feeling of strength, more of calm. You get it?"

"I don't know, but it sounds right. Wait a minute, I hear them talking in the kitchen. She'll be coming down. We can talk later. But know you have our support and it is much tougher now, even with the feeling of guilt." I heard her voice at the top of the stairs, then what sounded like a squeak and rapid steps down to where Jack was. "Here she is, Mark. Lor meet Mark!"

There was a pause and I knew she was taking the phone into the garage. The door came down and there was silence as if she'd disappeared. I didn't realize I was eating half the burrito until she answered, and I struggled to rapidly chew what was still in my mouth. I must have sounded like a washing machine. "Mark, you alright?"

"I'm eating a nuked burrito."

"Thank God, I thought you were drowning."

"No, I'm alive. You sound great."

"I wish I felt that way too."

"What?"

"I'm sorry I didn't want to see you." She was crying softly now.

"It was what it was, Lor. Let's not go back, okay?"

"Yeah. So, how are you?"

"A little awkward right now but I hope to snap out of it soon."

"Me too." I imagined she was smiling with the tears. "Listen, I… I'm shaking I'm so nervous right now. No more phone. You sleep, and I'll see you about noon."

"I'll be there."

"I love you even though I screwed up."

"I love you too." The phone went dead.

I settled back and stared at the fire again. The burrito was gone. The beer was empty. I let the sounds of the fire settle on me. A strange tense exhaustion finally caught up and I slept in my clothes under our quilt.

I was so used to waking to a green ceiling that the white above looked almost foreign for a moment until I realized again I was home, that we'd talked, that the connection was being made again, I hoped. I laid, still in my clothes, under the quilt. The only sound was a wind softer than at the lookout, and that white ceiling Lor and I had painted a year ago. I could even see the place where I'd applied too much. It looked like a white wort. She had pulled me down onto the bed in a lusty embrace. I had peeked again. How could so much seem ideal that hadn't been?

I tried to divert the fear that shot through my anxiety about the day to come by calling the PO and confirming I had my job, except now I'd have Donnie's forty-hour route until the bidding for it was complete. School would be starting back a week from Monday. But not for us. Maybe there'd be a 'reader's' job part-time in the department so I could keep my hand in until the next spring semester began. If we made it to spring. I tried to shake that off with a long shower. It was the old negative. Back from the woods, back to the ever negative me. But maybe less, I hoped.

I walked up to the little market on the Northside and got a pastry and huge coffee which I took to our tiny redwood deck by the tinier back yard which, bless him, Paul had kept mowed and trimmed. From there, the sun touched my back and I stared up into the hills, pretending to still be in the morning forest. I knew this was all avoidance and I kept avoiding by dusting, vacuuming and cleaning the kitchen and bathroom. But when it approached eleven, I knew I needed to go.

As I drove over the bay bridge I kept seeing her, at least imagining her: from the day she walked up out of nowhere in those cut-off Levi's and invited me to dinner to the day I went to work, and she didn't come home: images kept passing. What if this time it shattered her and these months away had changed her feelings, for whatever reason? She had had it all, to me: the beauty, the charm, humor and super intelligence that was deep, along with a bright mind. Just sitting with her was enough. And that crazy smile and wrinkled nose. And the compassion I knew I got from somewhere, a compassion which she had too. Everything.

chapter thirty-six

I turned down their street. Jack's truck was in the driveway. I barely made it up the stairs to the door before they were on the porch. First Mallie's hug, then Jack's. Lor looked at me with a tiny smile and we both hesitated for a second until she almost fell over into my embrace as I lifted her, and we twirled around. Mallie and Jack smiling was a blur through my tears. I didn't know where we were going, but the anxiety and fear withdrew almost completely.

Jack had opened a bottle of champagne and dear Mallie had made chicken salad sandwiches which we ate in the living room.

"She's real." Mallie smiled.

Lor's smile also had the wrinkled nose. "I don't think I'll break." Then she laughed as if the whole rehab had been a practical joke. She plopped down on the couch next to me and took my hand. "I'm not trying to make a joke, really."

"We're kind of pushing it, aren't we?" Jack asked of no one in particular, but we all nodded and let the gayness ease into more of a family quiet. "All right. Mallie and I are off to a movie and will be back around five. You two enjoy some privacy." Suddenly they were gone. Lor got up and got us each a beer and we sat for a long time in silence finishing the lunch.

"Do you think sitting's the answer?"

"No. How about we take a walk down to the beach?" She asked.

It was as if nothing happened or we were timid of speaking about the whole trauma and drama of the past months. We walked west past the strip mall with the storefront theatre where she had educated me on foreign films and down through more neighborhoods like hers until we crossed the highway into the parking lot and shore beyond. The late September sun hadn't gone into its winter slant yet and the light breeze was just cooling enough. That late, kids were already back in school, so we saw only old-timers with their dogs and a few surfers, their boards rising and falling in the disappointing waves. We headed south towards the zoo and the beach was even more deserted. I tried to hold her hand, but she only squeezed mine and let it drop. Any words seemed to be shattering. We kept up the silent pace for almost an hour. I didn't know what to say but was finished with the silence.

"I feel like a goldfish: exposed." I half laughed.

She tried a smile, and then another one. "I feel like the phony surrounding me." She kicked the sand.

"What?"

"Like anything I try to do now will have phony hoovering over it."

"You think we're all gonna' be walking on eggs, forever?"

She lurched over and kissed me dryly on the mouth but quickly continued our walk. "I just wanted you to know that was still there, but I won't feel very kissable for a while."

"I can wait. It's been months anyway. I'd like to hear us be honest, at least here where nobody can listen." I threw a rock into a wave and it disappeared.

"Okay. Let's begin with us. I want to come home. That's a start towards honesty."

This time we paused to gently but really kiss. I knew as we did that I still had the 'getting tough' part to get through.

chapter thirty-seven

I was back at work without school. We spent the first couple of weeks sort of 'sensing' each other out. It was delicate, but by week three the thaw was pretty much over. She didn't volunteer to see about some tutoring work in the math department and I didn't push. We would hug and kiss sometimes, but sex began to look like something from the past although I know we both had fleeting moments of tenderness that were clearly recognizable. Now everything was back in place, the cottage cleaned and almost beckoning us to come in as ourselves again. But before that happened, I got a phone call Sunday afternoon from out of the blue.

Such a call should have been my Mother but instead it was a longtime friend of hers from her work. Maybe it was that call that got Lor and I almost rattling around as the people we once were at summer's beginning before rehab.

Lor was on the couch and I'd just gotten us a glass of wine when the call came. By the way she talked, I knew it was for me… and weird. She mouthed 'for you,' and stuck out her tongue. At first, I thought it was my Mother but Lor shook her head and handed me the phone.

"Mark, this is Estelle, your mother's work friend."

"Hi?"

"She wanted me to call. Mark, your Grandmother died yesterday."

"Tell her thanks for letting me know but we were never close. Thanks for calling. Bye." I was this close to letting Estelle have it with both barrels. Why couldn't my Mother have called? Why would she think I gave a damn? But my experience at the lookout let the anger slide away. I was about to slam down the phone when Lor gently took it from me and pulled me onto the couch next to her. We just sat, our legs barely touching. Suddenly, with that experience, I wanted to pour out everything that I'd stored inside, including the thing I'd most avoided: the tough talk with Lor and where we were going.

I turned to her but didn't touch her. "I badly need to talk, Lor. And I think you do too."

"This is gonna be the big talk, isn't it?" She asked.

"I hope so. We let it all hang out and see who's standing when it's over."

"You want me to go first?" I could tell she didn't want to.

"Why don't we do a back and forth? We can start with my Mother."

She relaxed a little and nodded.

I moved away from her and leaned against the other arm, my feet up on the couch. "Alright, she couldn't even call me because she knew how I hated that old woman. And it's more than obvious now why none of her other kids wanted her and why my Mother was stuck with her out of some bullshit duty of guilt she had pounded into her. I've thought that maybe my Mother and I could have been even close if we'd been alone. Well, that's all gone now. Impossible. She was somebody else's mother, not mine."

I was crying then: bawling really. It wouldn't stop. Lor was crawling across the couch to console me but I raised my palms to stop her. I felt almost like an open sewer. It was pouring out. I felt as if I'd been running all day, but the shortness of breath was a relief. "We're truly a family of three plus your brother and sisters. That's it."

"But don't you think…?"

"Maybe when we're gray and old, but we…. I need to put all that pent-up grief aside."

"Do you want to keep going?"

"No, it's your turn." I could have given her a long, gentle soul kiss if we'd been closer, but didn't move. Lor sat up and re-crossed her legs. She'd already put on her winter wool pajamas. I signaled her to hold on while I lit the fire. It was still light outside.

She took some slow, relaxed yoga breaths before she began. "This is really all about me. Wait, don't say anything yet. I know it's about us, but I had a long time to think about us without 'we,' which means without me. You understand? Good." She paused for another couple of breaths. "I won't screw up again. We're fine. Isn't it as simple as that?"

"Whoa, now. Not that simple."

"Why?"

"My turn again?" She sunk down and rested her head on the back of the couch. "Thank you. And I understand your brief summary, but there's a little more." I knew that Mallie and Jack had given her the 'tough talk' but when I looked at her, so focused on me, I didn't know how to begin it. I started to get up but realize the wine was poured; it was no longer an excuse.

"They already told you, right?"

"Yeah."

"Then, Mark it really is that simple. I'm the whole focus, and you know that"

"They told me you guys had this talk and when you say something like that, I somehow think it was lost in translation with you and them. Why? Because you aren't the whole focus. There're four of us, not just you. I think you know that, right?"

"I… look I'm sorry, I didn't mean it to come out wise-assed or snotty. Yes, I do know that."

"Okay, then let me share my thoughts." I looked at her a full minute before speaking. It was now, one way or the other. "This could be called the hardball shit I think, and neither of us like it because this could end us." Lor slowly nodded and nervously pushed back her corn rows with both hands. "My love, you have put us through some tough times, your parents more than me but we must come to terms with it now, like it or not."

"I agree."

"It's not a matter of judging you on what you do, but they can't afford it anymore and I just can't live with it. How someone who had been raised with so much love, love I never knew or was ever conscious of, can have this "unrelenting despair" overcome you is beyond any understanding I can bring to it, especially since it turns into self-destruction instead of learning and stopping. So only you seem to get it. But we don't. And that would be tragic because you're surrounded by love. Because you are so damned loveable, don't you know that?" She nodded again but I could see the tears. "Then just try and let us love you every time this horrible cloud rises. Please." I moved across the couch and held her without speaking. The new fire had taken hold and the room was warming. Then our embrace ended but she nestled her head on my shoulder and slowly rubbed my back until she reached up, kissed my cheek like a sister might, and let go.

"Thank you for that, Mark. Keep talking."

chapter thirty-eight

We didn't make love that night nor talk more. In fact, the next day, Monday, we hardly talked at all. Yet it didn't feel like anything had to be said by the time I went to work in the late afternoon.

When I got home around 9:30, she was still up and had built another fire. She'd made her famous spaghetti and meat-mushroom sauce. We sipped bourbon by the fire before dinner and the silence continued until we were back by the fire with the Modern Jazz Quartet playing softly. I noticed that Lor had spread out some math papers and a couple of books on our shared deck, but they look just pushed there like she was forcing herself to deal with them.

"Why the math stuff?"

She got up and poured a little bourbon in our coffees. "Just messing around, I guess. Seems like a hundred years ago that I looked at it."

"You don't have to…"

"No, I want to. It showed me my brain still seems to function well." She smiled for the first time since I had come in.

"But not too interested, I assume?" I ventured.

She collapsed on the other side of the couch. "Sort of…. but more than that too." She hesitated. "I've been having the 'why bother' thoughts off and on since I've been home. Like what does it all lead to anyway?"

"Honestly, that's what a lot of my work time has been spent thinking. What've we got? You could be starting an MA and me a Ph. D. What does it lead to? Maybe a house, a college town, an office and the coming and going. I know what you mean more than you may think. See, I kind of did my own rehab. while you were gone. I'm guilty also of that old 'unrelenting despair.' We may have gotten it in different ways but got it anyway."

Lor crawled across the couch and lay her head on my legs with her face towards the ceiling. It was such a surprise that I don't think either of us realized it at first. I let my hand weave softly through her corn rows. I think we were both contemplating that shift because we stayed there until the fire needed more wood. When she got up, she pulled her legs in cross-legged and pressed against me. Our faces weren't very far apart. She leaned forward, and we kissed, the most real kiss since she'd come home: soft, slow, pressing and not fleeting.

"So, the way I get it is we're working on the same thing from different angles?"

"Yeah, that sounds right to me."

She kissed my lips with her tongue. "You're saying we're both working it out: you from a dead childhood and me from something I can't tell where it comes from?"

"What you're really wanting to say is that you're no longer the center of all our fear that it could happen again because I'm now in there too, also trying to work it out... whatever 'it' is." We did another real kiss and her body was pressing into mine almost like when it began.

"I like that, Marco, mi amigo." She was nestling in my arms then.

"Yes, yes. It's like Gary Snyder once said in a poem, *you move a single board and the rain stops coming in.*"

"Yeah!" she was almost gleeful. "I don't have to feel the fear of failing." I nodded and tweaked her nose. "Can we make love again? I'll try to be naked with just one candle burning."

Our lives returned more rapidly from then on, but somehow, we hadn't talked about my experience at the lookout. The feeling came and went as I worked and walked my route but seemed to have been buried under this huge wave of emotion of having Lor home again. I also think I purposefully didn't bring it up I feared she would view it as a separation after we had finally begun to heal.

By Christmas, it was gratefully another world for all of us. We had Mallie and Jack over for a community-cooked meal since they were alone. We even had to force them to relax and stay over through the day after Christmas.

As the months passed, I'd like to say it was magic. But it wasn't. We seemed to be growing closer by the day.

By the time spring break came (we were still on school time), Lor was back to her tutoring and was again assured a slot in the master's program beginning in the summer and I'd been thinking about the Ph.D.. in literature more than I ever had. Maybe we were academics, though we hated the thought every time it came up in conversation.

We had both had so many uncaring, egocentric, arrogant types between us as teachers that it was hard to conceive of more years of that and finally ending in the middle of it all if we could find jobs. We rationalized that graduate school faculty had a closer and more caring relationship with its students.

She really appeared to be happy just being about half domestic, and my working 40 hours a week paid the bills and was mounting our savings far beyond what I could have imagined. Yet we had also had amazing breakthroughs. First, the poet's *"unrelenting despair"* had dramatically retreated in our lives. She even demanded we test this on occasion and I accompanied her to North Beach which had always been a place of rekindling her past.

She even talked to a couple people on the street who she knew that still looked partially alive. But I truly worried the times we did this that she would come away with negatives that I could perceive. Her remarks riding home gave me the feeling that she now felt foreign in such a world and wondered aloud how she'd ever gotten there. If 'despair' arose, we shared it because it had touched us both and mutual support kept us in that state for diminishing amounts of time.

The second dramatic presence in our lives came forward and embraced us. It was the one bond of trust that had remained out of reach until she came home this time; it was her suggestion of candlelight as we made love when we again reembraced. To me, it was the last hang-up from the past. And it was much more than physical.

More and more, the candle remained, and she wasn't shying away from it. In fact, there were nights she'd surprise me in different places—the living room, the bathroom door—standing, luring, tempting me with subtle and not so subtle moves: naked in the light. What an incredible gesture after what she had endured. The first time I cried but managed to hide it from her.

In all these months we had not talked about my experience in the woods. I don't know why I felt it would separate us except that I had had the experience and I imagined she had not. Then, one night during the Easter school break, the weather turned suddenly warm and we decided to eat on our small desk in the back yard. It was a quiet Sunday which had left us feeling mellow. She had put together a small leg of lamb with scalloped potatoes and peas. We were drinking some white wine before dinner.

"Since I've come home I can feel a real peace, but I don't know where it comes from."

"Maybe just accept it, don't analyze it."

Lor smiled so easily. "Mark, be honest. You want to tell me something? I could feel it all day and for weeks but didn't want to push."

"I'll never stop being amazed how we do that to each other."

"Well?"

"It's about an experience I had at the lookout that we've not talked about."

"Why haven't we?" I moved closer to her and touched her face. "Is it so serious?" She asked.

"I not sure, that's why I never brought it up. I guess I thought it was."

"After what we've just come through, it can't be that earth-shaking, can it?"

"I guess we'll see." I moved back to my end of the bench.

"Have you ever wondered whether we really know what's real and what's not?"

She crinkled her nose and I knew a bombshell was coming.

"You mean like my parents always do when politics come up? They can't talk about it, it upsets them so much?"

I shook my head. "And why?"

"Because they're disgusted every time there's an election and fools and crooks, from the President down, win elections. They can't believe we can be so naïve and stupid as a country to vote for them, pretending they stand for some kind of 'American values' when, if anyone dug a little deeper, they'd see these types for what they are."

"Right, but who's supposed to do the 'deep digging?'"

Lor tightened her lips and gave me this look like I'd been standing behind the door the day they gave out brains. "We both know that. The media, from hometown newspapers to big time New York news anchors."

"But if you really listen to them, they seldom if ever dig deep enough. They rarely truly, critically analyze the stories they report. Take the Watts disaster. They reported the fires and shootings and lootings and police and citizen fights, but few reports questioned the people who were in the center of it all. Those stopped for an alleged traffic violation. Yeah, there was a little of that and lots of talk of being poor and desperate, talk of revising the police and rebuilding and education plans. And then it all vanished from the news. Just isolated incidents came and went and the conclusion I was left with was that that community was full of troublemakers, and what about all the civil rights they got in the mid-sixties? Why does Watts probably still look a lot like it did during the riots, except for some shallow window dressing?"

291

"I get it and I don't know why." We drank some beer in unison.

"Me either. That in a roundabout way leads back to my lookout experience. I'll describe it first, so you can get some of the feeling for the place. You want me to go on?"

"It's the only thing we haven't talked about since I came home." Lor squinted at me. "What do you think, Mark?"

"Okay, bear with me."

"Where am I going?"

"Yes. Well it was like this." She was smiling, and I smiled back. "I drank a lot the first month. I'd never felt that alone except when I was a kid at home. Just nothing but me and silence except for the radio reports to headquarters. But in the second month, I began getting out, looking around. I also admit I had some fear since they'd told me the area had some mountain lions, bobcats and bears—none of which I ever saw near the lookout.

"There was a log carved into two seats about thirty yards from the tower, and I finally ventured over there and sat for a while. It took in a view that went north to the crater and east over the forest and a couple ranges of mountains. For some reason, it really held me. I swear, after a while I felt like there was a veil between me and the world and the more I stared, the harder time I had identifying with the world that you and Jack and Mallie made up. It was almost like you all had vanished. I finally went back to the tower and had two or three heavy shots of bourbon and that put me at the desk where I called in my early evening report. Sitting there afterwards and trying to decide what was for dinner, I really noticed the stream down beyond the log chair a couple hundred yards down a steep incline. It was still full of run off, even though we were well into summer. Like I said, it was twilight, and to my surprise some of the forest animals were there having an evening drink. What amazed me was that they weren't going after each other: just drinking. By the time I climbed down from the tower and made my dinner and bought it upstairs again, they were gone; only the stream was left.

"Anyway, from then on I got friendlier with the forest. I took longer walks between readings; I finished all the books I'd bought with me. Even read some of them more than once. But I kept going back to the forest and everything that accompanied it: the sky, the crater, my stream of twilight drinkers. I wasn't learning anything new in those books, so I spent more time between radio calls either hiking (I even got halfway down to the stream) or sitting in my double-chaired log and letting my gaze drift over the forest.

"I remember one night checking the calendar and figuring I had six weeks left. I'd almost missed a report in that day since I'd gone further than ever into the deep woods and I was tired. I got in bed sometime around nine because the summer light had disappeared from my windows. All day, my mind seemed tormented by a mire of thoughts about what the hell I was going to do, what were we going to do, would you make it this time, could I be tough with you? It was like a nightmare in broad daylight. And it was still there, even with a coax to remove it by some stiff drinks.

"I'd been tired but was fully awake. I tossed and turned until about three-thirty. Getting up, I thought a drink would help but the idea didn't go anywhere. I was fully dressed except for my shoes, so I put them on along with my coat and hat and went downstairs where I woke up completely with a douse of cold water in a washcloth across my face and hands.

"Then I bundled up and went out into the darkness. It was coming up on four. By now, I knew my way blindfolded over and down to the log chairs. I watched the shadows of the moon touching the stream and the trees down in front of me. I don't know how long I was there, but eventually my thoughts were quiet and I relaxed against the wood.

"The sky lit up slowly to my east and the sun lifted into dawn, making me shield my eyes and look down toward the stream. Animals were already at the stream. I couldn't hear the water but imagined it. The first sun was directly in my eyes by now and the forest appeared to be on fire in the tallest leaves and branches. But I know it wasn't. I looked back down to the animals and stared at them until the last had taken a drink and left the stream. I practically had to pry myself up from the log and staggered back to the lookout. I managed to make my first report, then dropped onto the bed and slept.

"The radio woke me. I hadn't called in the second report. I laid there staring at that green wood ceiling almost until it was time for the third call. I was just staring, no thoughts. I felt at peace like I'd never felt before. I sort of stumbled around the next five days. I was either at the desk or down at the log but always staring. Sometimes I traced the sun's light off the crater, and through the leaves as it followed each day until I had to go back to call in a report or cobble together something to eat. I must have lost five pounds. But I wasn't hungry. I didn't drink. Only peace and staring.

"On the sixth day, I had to snap out of it when I heard the horse coming up with the supplies. I guess I talked okay to the ranger. Luckily, he was new, and we'd never met so I must have gotten through it. I thought about it but couldn't figure out what had happened. All I knew was that I'd come through some kind of experience and its feeling of peace remained strong. The only word that made any sense out of it was 'seeing.' Like I'd never really seen. My thoughts, my judgements, my fears and doubts: nothing fazed me, they just flowed past when I closed my eyes." I reached over and put my hands on top of hers. "I somehow gave up on everything and it didn't matter. I'm still feeling that peace, that seeing. Less now but still there. I can live in the world and yet it continues." I stopped talking and nodded at her.

Lor was smiling but looking intensely at me. "I wish I had something like that." She bent down and kissed both of my hands and laid her head on them. "You could have told me before, when you first got home. It couldn't separate us. I wasn't scared. It felt soft and easy to me, honest." She sat and looked to our north at the Berkeley hills, then back at me. "It had to be a spiritual moment, Mark." She said it so straight and without apology.

"That's a hard one to believe, Lor. How could some twenty-four-year-old have an experience that people across the globe use their whole life searching for and never find?" She didn't reply. "It's too impossible, Lor. But I can still feel the peace and close my eyes and make out the forest."

Nothing was said as we finished our dinner and went back inside. I lit a fire and she bought us each a glass of red wine. Then we sat and stared at the fire awhile. I kept wishing she'd speak.

"But how does that reality connect to the one you were talking about? I don't understand. It sounds like the forest was real, but our living isn't? That doesn't make any sense."

"I thought about that from the day it happened until I left the lookout. It hung on, but not in a negative way. It hung on like peace and never bugged me. I still don't know the answer. I confess, I even talked to God out in the silence, but I haven't heard anything yet. All I can tell you is what I think right now." The fire was warming the room now. She gave me a gentle thumbs-up. "All right, I'll do my best."

"What we have been trained to believe is real is what we have counted on and haven't thought too much about it. We've accepted school, job, family or alone, death. But have you ever wondered if there's something we haven't tapped into. Something we haven't seen that would open to another and better reality? Wasn't that partly what the sixties was; finding what was real for you? Wasn't that how the drugs came into it? Searching for your own way of giving? Something you wanted to do? Our reality now is just up to this moment and what we do with it from now on doesn't have to be the same. What's our adventure? A Ph.D.. is not really any adventure, any life I really need right now. Sure, it may look the safest and easiest. How about you, an MA in math? Is that the decision you truly want to make right now?"

She moved closer to me on the couch. "Honestly? I'm afraid, given my past history, that I'd go off the deep end again if I looked for the reality I want."

"Me too, Lor. Now we're safe and it's not scary. And I want something too, but it blows my mind."

Her arm nearly knocked me off the couch she got so close suddenly. "I got it! I got it!" She pounded me and the couch and kept banging up against me.

"Easy on me, huh?"

"I'm sorry, but I got it! I never thought about it!"

"What?"

"That's how I got into drugs in the first place! I was happy but bored being a good kid. It's not that I wanted to be bad. I just needed more. I went to a friend for the weekend. She had these mushrooms from some place and I was afraid to eat much but it gave me my own kind of peace and this need to figure out what this good kid really was. Yes, I know I went too far and never found much but a dead feeling in the heroin. But it will grab you. Though not like your experience. You know the rest."

She was still fidgeting but I had my arm wrapped around her. "You were questing." She shook her head 'yes.' I couldn't speak for a few seconds. It was like taking a body blow, but one that did no harm. "God! I've been doing the same thing since childhood and didn't know it. My forest experience was one end to a long search I didn't know I was making." I settled back on the couch and she settled into me. This was about as good as the forest experience and I couldn't stop grinning.

"Sure. The military, Dino, school, the psychic, the reading, meditating and thinking, everything else, Mark."

"Only fear stops choice." I said to the flames. "My reality."

"And mind."

"Yeah…yes." I turned to face her. "So, do you want to go first?"

"It's pretty simple. I want to walk next to the Seine, drink espresso for breakfast in a sidewalk café, eat lunch in the park, see all the museums; one big cliché and not very original, but I love it." She gave me this sexy glance. "And make love" Another smile. "Tell me yours now."

"Lor, I honestly don't have one. My lookout experience was the gift of a new reality. Nothing I saw had I ever seen before. Yet I'd seen it all before many times. The greatest gift I got was a feeling that I had given up. Washing everything out of me, flowing by, no pulling me into shit. Just flowing along. And I'm not fighting to maintain it, letting it be. You understand?"

"I hope so. But I kind of doubt it."

"Let's talk about making the real, *real*." She lay the length of the couch with her feet across my legs. "We've been bummed by what's called real: math, school, good job, security. We've kept it a secret from each other. Oh, yeah, we've talked and complained about it before and since we've been together, but what have we done? Me, I went the status quo except for jail and so did you, except for some little detours. Yet whatever way we went, I think we were motivated by the same thing, this old 'unrelenting despair' that rises and falls but remains part of our lives. This we have in common?"

I could barely hear her whisper, 'yes.'

"Do you want to step in and add something?" A half smile I guess meant she wanted me to keep talking. "Ok, I'll keep talking. So that brings us out of any alienation we might have had between your search and mine. Jack and Mallie are over there but they want what's best for us without trying to name it or push us into anything."

"That feels comfortable." She laid her head back on the arm of the couch.

"Is our purpose worrying about dropping into the status again, or is it trying to find how we got there and how we get the hell out and find real?"

"Or maybe go in further but through a different door?" Lor asked but I didn't answer because I didn't have a clue what she meant.

"Yeah, alright. Down deep where we don't want to go right now, or maybe never…?"

"A los pobres, los ricos que comein merde!" She blurted out of nowhere.

"What?"

"Sorry. I was thinking, 'here's to the poor, may the rich eat shit.'"

"How does that fit in?"

"I was just thinking about a world of abundance with poverty everywhere. As close as right down the hill in Oakland."

"I still don't get it."

"How often have we talked about the injustices of it? But always just talk?"

"So?"

"We're just airing out aren't we, putting ourselves on the table like? We find almost a hopelessness in what we've been doing. I just thought what it would be like being poorer than we are or even working for the poor."

"In early 1600's, John Winthrop, governor of Massachusetts Bay, said something to the effect 'God had divined that there would always be rich and poor.' But Zen says that when you feed the poor without any judgement of how they got there, that it's not food you are giving them but an awareness. Don't ask me what that means, I read it ten times and didn't get it. Your thought is great, but can I keep going and then we can look at that?" She gave me her anger grin, her lips pulled apart, which was a kind of 'fuck you' and 'go ahead' combined. "I can only see us as stuck. I'm sick of the PO and truthfully, sick of school but what choices do we have but keep on the same track?"

This time she sat up. "We also have six thousand and interest saved."

I interjected, "But we were giving some of that to Jack and Mallie for the rehab."

"Well, we could start with a thousand for the rehab and pay off the rest monthly or something like that. I know they'd be okay with that."

"Ah, not exactly, I... I was going to spent about eighteen hundred." She looked at me questioningly. "Please, you gotta trust me, it's really important." She reluctantly nodded. "What did you have in mind for the rest?"

She moved closer and started nervously running her hand up my leg. "You've gotta trust me." We just looked at each other. "Oh, the hell with secrets. Why shouldn't I tell you? I really meant it when I talked about going to Europe, not just Paris but all over. When you think about it, what do we have to lose?"

"Oh, just my position for a Ph.D.. and you for the MA. I doubt if they would let us have another extension that easy."

"I know, and it scares me, Mark, but I like the idea. A few months, a different perspective, different ideas and people. And we're young. Jack and Mallie have always regretted not doing something like that when they were young. I think we'd have their blessing. And you could teach me how to meditate or something too. You've still got the feeling from the forest."

"I like the idea. But where would we be when we get back?"

"I don't know. Maybe a cabin in the Maine woods, I don't know."

"So, we give up everything we've done so far, give up?"

"What an idea." She laughed. "But are we too afraid to give up? What if the money runs out?"

"You speak some bad French from high school and me, excellent Spanish. I think we'd get along out in another world."

"Can we sleep on it?" God, I never realized she was so up for the idea.

"I think we'll be talking part or most of the night."

Let's get comfortable by the fire and have another glass of wine." She got up, pressed against me and gave me a polite, gentle kiss before going for the wine.

chapter thirty-nine

The idea kept bouncing back and forth, up and down pretty much the whole night until we dropped off around five. It was Sunday and there were no schedules to meet, no demands for the next week like when we were in school. About ten, we began to move around, and I watched Lor, completely without hesitance, get up and go naked to the bathroom, twitching in mock sexiness and laughing as she went. It was one of those unexpected love moments you never forget, considering what she'd come through.

When she came back, she gave me this sexy exposure that made us both laugh, and we laid back in bed with smiles at the ceiling until the phone rang. I answered.

"How does baked chicken in my special sauce, gravy, potatoes and string beans sound for a Sunday dinner?" Mallie asked.

"Really more than perfect." I motioned a thumbs-up to Lor. "We'll bring the wine and desert if that's okay?"

"Sounds great. Around four. Now can I talk to your girl-woman." She laughed as I handed the phone to Lor who immediately launched into one of their typically long Mom and Daughter talks. I got up and had breakfast ready by the time she came out and was reading the paper by one of the front windows in the living room.

"So?"

"Great." Anticipating my hesitance about breaking our night long news to them, I could feel her words being measured. "I….," she paused, and I had to look at her to make her go on. "Are you sure?"

"I could ask you the same. Yes, positively." She came over and hugged me.

"We'll be okay?"

"Again, I believe you."

"Then this has to be a good time to tell them. We'll also present them with the first thousand payment going toward the rehab debt." She was about to speak more in doubt than fear and I cut in. "We give up, Lor! Sweetheart, we do. Yes!

We didn't even reassure each other on the way over. We watched the late March sky give us a crystal blue Sunday as we drove across the bridge through the afternoon traffic. When we got to their street in the avenues, the late winter light was slowly fading.

As always, they greeted us with warmth on the high front steps and led us into the living room. Jack poured spirits all around and we sat by an early fire. Mallie laid the whole thing open before we had spoken a dozen words to each other.

She looked doubtfully at Lor and asked, "Taylor, what are you so itchy about?"

And she never hesitated. "Mark and I have some plans we want to share with you."

I interrupted, "First." I took out the thousand-dollar check and handed it to both of them. "This is our first of many payments to come to help pay down this family debt. And that's how we look at it." They studied the check. Mallie was going to cry but stopped with a smiled instead. They almost said 'thank you' in unison.

I raised my hand. "We can't tell you when the next one will come, but it will."

"Can I finish now?" Lor exclaimed. Everyone pointed at her and laughed. "Okay, as I said, we have a plan we've been talking through and thinking about for some time, so it's not just a spur of the moment thing."

Jack settled back next to Mallie and sipped his beer. "We'd love to hear it and, no, we would never assume spur of the moment since I think we both get the impression that it's pretty serious."

Lor glanced at me but I motioned for her to continue as we'd agreed.

"We just aren't ready to continue for higher degrees. In fact, we're tired of school. It's become somewhat meaningless to us."

"You don't plan to go to graduate school for now?" Jack asked with a very slight look of surprise on his face. Mallie too.

"That's right, Dad. We feel we need something new."

"A new landscape." I interjected.

"What do you guys propose?" Mallie asked. "Oh, oh, I think I can feel it coming." She looked at Jack.

Lor jumped in again. "We've saved enough to take a trip and have decided to get Euro passes and rucksacks, and travel around Europe and Britain, etc. We want to do...."

Jack interrupted. "I'll say it. Like your Mom and I always planned to do but somehow never got around to doing?"

Now Lor and I both nodded in unison. "We don't know how long we'd be gone but we really want to do it like you both have said, while we still can. And you know we're sorry you two never went," She said.

The last was almost a plea of forgiveness but it was heartfelt. The suspense was over. It was done. I got up and hugged Lor. "So...what do you think?"

They looked at each other before Jack spoke. "Well, we'll worry like hell about you and wish you were doing it married and worry about what you'll do when you get back to make a living."

"And worry about me and drugs?" Lor hesitantly questioned.

"Taylor, that's not fair." Mallie said.

"Sure it is, Mom. But I can't expect you not to. Mark and I realize that we've got a lot of the same challenges, in different ways. And have acted them out in different ways but we gotta' try, you know?" They suddenly came across the room and embraced us both. I could feel real affirmation for one of the few times in my life.

The evening was spent talking over what we'd see and listening to their suggestions. The longer we talked, the better it sounded to all of us. I was giving plenty of notice on my job and so was Lor. We parted and set a date for dinner the night before we were flying to England.

On the way home, Lor and I were quiet except for some sighs and giggles. We were really beginning to believe in our own adventure and figured we had enough money to be gone at least all summer starting in May. When we got home, we sat by a fire and looked at the brochures I'd collected. Then I grabbed them away. "We'll do it on our own, no guides but some maps."

Out of nowhere she said, "I'll make it, Mark."

I kissed her cheek. "I never thought you wouldn't. Remember you asked about the eighteen hundred I took from our account? Well, I think you are game for my surprise, but I didn't want to worry your folks about it."

"What."

"I hope you agree?"

"Come on."

"I found this service where you can pick up a motor scooter in Europe when we get there. It wouldn't happen until we hit Europe. I figured we'd rent a car and drive through the Isles first. The travel people said B&Bs aren't too crowded in May, so we'd drive up through Ireland, Scotland and all and then back and take the ferry over to France. This service even tells us the right gear we'll need for our trip and gets it for us at discounts, when we pick up the scooter. They've got it down to a science, so we won't be overloaded"

She looked a little perplexed. "What's this secret vehicle you spent our money on?"

I leaned over and gave her a soft kiss. "Are you sure you're ready?"

"Yes, for god's sake, yes."

"A Vespa!"

The End

About the Author

 I was born in a manger, actually a large and sturdy cardboard box filled with straw, in an alley next to the main L.A. railroad station. I never knew my parents because I heard it whispered that the birth was divine, and my parents were forced to leave town under cover of darkness. I played with others like myself in and around the station and attended the school the railroad ran in exchange for carrying railroad luggage 10 hours a day for two bowls of rice and some greens. I was suddenly adopted by a world-famous writer whose "writer's block" I filled for 20 years, learning the craft that would pester me to this day. Eventually, I managed to find a wonderful woman and we started a family by the sea where we remain. If you need any further information please use highway 101 phone box number 348 about 10 miles north of Goleta, Ca.

www.ingramcontent.com/pod-product-compliance
Lightning Source LLC
Chambersburg PA
CBHW051241260626
47162CB00002B/542